Violette Kee-Tui

Mulberry Dreams

Pigeon Press

Published by Pigeon Press

12 Fortune's Gate Road, Bulawayo, Zimbabwe

For more information on this and other titles email:
info@hubbardstours.com

Cover: Blessing Chakandinakira
Cover Design: Wayne Nel
Text Design & Typesetting: Wayne Nel

ISBN 978-1-77906-145-4

To Emil and Katya,
who believed in me
when I didn't believe in myself.

ACKNOWLEDGEMENTS

I'VE IMAGINED WRITING an acknowledgements page ever since it started to become a very real possibility that *Mulberry Dreams* would be published. And it's really only happening now not due to my own efforts, but to so many along the way who have helped, advised, supported and gently (and not so gently) prodded me. Chief among the "prodders" is Paul Hubbard who probably asked me at least three times a week, over a period of three months and usually out of context when we were talking about something completely different, where my book was. It proves the theory that it is possible to frustrate someone into action! I'm extremely grateful to him not only for his support for *Mulberry Dreams* and his offer to publish it, but for being a partner in every sense of the word. Thank you, also, to admired writer and my dear friend, John Eppel, who took the time to edit it and offer advice on various changes. Encouragement from a writer of his calibre was an honour I will never take lightly. Thank you so much to my friend and colleague over the years, Wayne Nel, who, during a discussion on another design job, learnt about my book and insisted I get it done. He offered to typeset it as a favour, to get me going – and it worked! When I first saw

Mulberry Dreams typeset as a book, I was over the moon! My friend, Blessing Chakandinakira, then painted the beautiful cover for me and the book, in my head anyway, was complete. Apart from another 100 or so edits! Thank you to my family who have been unbelievably supportive of my writing, from the time, as a shy, mousey 15 year old I declared I wanted to be a journalist, through my transition into fiction writing and now the publication of *Mulberry Dreams*. I apologise in advance, Mom and Dad, for the, at times, salty language – when the strongest word we ever used in our childhood home was "dammit"! Thank you to Thom Vernon, my brother-in-law and a highly-acclaimed published author and lecturer, who gave me my first ever opportunity to read my work out loud alongside his during a family reunion in Sarasota – and to all my family who offered their support and encouragement of it. I reserve the best for last: my darling children, Emil and Katya, to whom I've dedicated this book. In the throes of writing the first draft, I may have for a time become an absentee parent, so caught up was I in this other imaginary world I was creating. Thank you for giving me the freedom to explore that part of me, for understanding I am your mother but many other things as well. And thank you, Katya, for being one of my first reviewers, aged 14. Unbeknown to you, I had sent you a censored version, minus the bad language and sexual innuendo ("darn" and "bloody" featured a lot in the heated dialogue!) and you loved it. I hope you still love it in its finished form!

CHAPTER ONE

Emma 1978

THE LAST TIME Daddy went back to the army I made him mad, but I didn't mean to. He was wearing his army uniform and I thought he looked very smart but very serious, and he was sitting really, really straight in the driver's seat of the green van from the army. I could see his chin just over the top of the steering wheel and, without moving his head, just his eyes, he was checking this way and that, and then this way and that again, in his side mirrors as he reversed up our driveway. It was a pretty long driveway and Mommy used to turn her head all the way around to check and then Daddy would shout.

You don't need to turn your whole head around, Daddy would say in his bossy voice. Use your side mirrors. That's what they're there for! Mommy would just smile, but only with her mouth, and keep turning her head round.

That day, the last day, we were all outside saying good-bye to him: Mommy, Peter and I. When he started up the engine, Peter and Mommy walked back into the house but I didn't. I remembered about my birthday. So I ran down the driveway after him, waving my arms over my head to make him stop.

He stopped but he looked grumpy when I ran to his open window. It was hot and I don't run so well, not fast like Peter. So I was kinda out of breath when I got to him.

What is it Emma? he asked, and I was already thinking, from the look on his face and his voice, that I shouldn't have come.

Daddy, it's my birthday next week, I said, trying to catch my breath while I said it.

Yes, Emma, he said, I know that it's your birthday, and he sighed so I knew he was getting impatient, and I tried to be quick, spilling all my words out in a big hurry.

Are you gonna be home for it, Daddy? I asked him. I'm gonna be 10. Tell the army to let you have time off so you can come.

Daddy rolled his eyes and said, Emma, if the army gave time off for every birthday, anniversary and tea party, how do you imagine this war would get won?

I wasn't really thinking about war right then, just my birthday.

Oh. I said. I wasn't sure what to say next so I asked him again to try, to please, please try to be back.

He didn't say anything, he just held onto the steering wheel and started moving his eyes this way and that, and I knew he was getting ready to reverse.

He looked oh so serious. I didn't want him to look like that, really serious and worried and kind of sad. So I put my hand on his arm and he looked around at me and that's when I said what I said about Harry.

I didn't know he was mad at first, coz he didn't say anything for a little while. But when he spoke his voice was low, like it was coming from deep inside his chest, and tight like the strings on Peter's guitar. Step away from the car, Emma, he said. I'm late. He was holding so tightly onto the steering wheel, I saw his knuckles were white. Then he started to reverse again.

I stepped back so quickly I almost fell. I wasn't feeling happy and excited about my birthday anymore.

I turned to walk back down the driveway to the house and to Peter and Mommy when I heard the screeching sound. I felt it deep in my tummy. I swung around and saw that the side of the van, just by the part with the lights that always reminded Peter and me of a frowning face, was pushed up hard against the gate. Daddy had crashed.

But he didn't get out of the car to check. He didn't even stop. I saw him turn the steering wheel really hard and then he sped fast out on to the street. I could hear the engine whirring for a really long time while he drove away.

CHAPTER
TWO

IN A SECOND everything can change. For Emma that second came two weeks after her father smashed into the gate, the day before her 10th birthday. The second she heard the gun shot.

She didn't know what it was, the loud explosion that tore through the still afternoon and made both children jump in the back seat of the car. But Peter, who went hunting on his friend Jim's farm all the time, did. He'd told Emma all about it as they sat side-by-side in the mulberry tree in the back yard.

"It's loud! It makes a big crack and your ears ring," he said, whittling away at a branch with a pen knife.

"Were you scared?" she asked.

"Nah," he said, not taking his eyes off the branch. He was lying, and she knew it, but secrets and lies and fears were all somehow safe in the mulberry tree.

It was a massive tree, so tall and wide they could climb right up into its leafy branches and perch on its wide limbs. Under its green shelter, they'd once hidden away in their own private world, eating mulberries until their hands and faces were tattooed a deep mauve, their stomachs aching. It was the setting of all their childhood games, the backdrop of their magical fantasy land.

Then everything had changed. Everything, it seemed, except the tree. Standing looking at it today, Emma felt the ache of memory press on her chest. It had been, unbelievably, almost 30 years since she'd last stood at the foot of the tree and climbed its branches, confident in the belief that up there nothing could harm her.

But it didn't take her long to realise there were no safe places, to realise that even as they sat in their innocent little bubble in the mulberry tree throughout that last, gloriously blue summer, a war had been raging around them. And maybe they'd have heard it if they hadn't been giggling so loudly.

When her world fell apart again two months ago, all she wanted to do was come back.

Getting here hadn't been easy; when she told Daniel she was going home, he thought she meant Seattle where they'd met...he had no idea she was going back not 10 years but 30, to a time and place he knew nothing about.

Then the letter from Wallace and Hogg, the advertising agency where she'd been working as an accountant for the last eight years. Emma was being retrenched; she was the only one of the 40 employees who celebrated that day.

She used her retrenchment package, from a job she'd started to hate, to buy a ticket direct from New York to Johannesburg, then on to Bulawayo.

As the 737 made a bumpy landing on the long, grey tarmac, cut like a gash through the emerald treetops, Emma wept with relief.

She had tears running down her face again now, looking up at the mulberry tree, maybe not as tall as she remembered but still, in a funny way, her sanctuary.

No therapist – and she'd been to a few – could ever understand how to help her because they hadn't known how it had started. And neither could Daniel.

There was no-one who could but Peter, and how she wished he was back here with her now. Maybe if he was, if they could somehow turn back the hands of time, it would all be OK again.

"Can I help you?" A voice startled her back to the present and she swung around to see a wizened face, staring at her from under a thatch of grey hair.

"Oh! I'm so sorry!" she said, drying tears which had left her face feeling sticky and tight. "I rang the bell at the gate; a gardener let me in."

The woman continued to look at her, brow furrowed, lips pursed.

"I used to live here, I grew up in this house," said Emma. "I'm so sorry; I just wanted to see it again."

"You grew up here, dear?" asked the old woman, her head tilted.

"I've been gone so long," she said, almost by way of apology and, all at once, she felt she didn't know herself any better than this stranger standing in front of her, that everything about her was as alien as the accent that had crept into her speech.

"How long ago did you leave?" the old woman asked, still staring at her.

"Thirty years."

"And your name is…?"

"Emma, Emma Groves, but I was a Hardy back then."

"Hardy? Margot Hardy's child?" The old woman's eyes narrowed.

"Yes, you knew her?"

"Knew of her. I'm sorry my child…"

And, suddenly, she felt every bit a child again.

She felt dizzy, overcome with floods of memories, snatches of vintage film she'd stored away such a long time ago she was surprised she could still see them so clearly. The blood, the screaming, Peter grabbing her arm and spinning her away from the scene, burying her head in his shoulder so she wouldn't see. Harry howling like a wounded animal.

"I think I need to sit down," she said. And the next thing, she was falling, falling through space, falling through ages, falling and nothing there to catch her.

CHAPTER
THREE

AT FIRST SHE HAD no idea where she was. But as her vision and her brain cleared, she recognized her old bedroom.

Then it all started coming back to her: the tree, the old woman, falling for what seemed like forever. She felt a stab of pain on her arm and looked down to see bruises that had already percolated to a deep mulberry. A bump on her head made her feel giddy when she touched it.

She sat up slowly and swung her legs onto the floor.

She looked around for her shoes but they were nowhere in sight so she padded, barefoot, out of the bedroom and down the familiar corridor – the tiny bathroom and toilet on one end, the lounge-cum-dining room on the other – running her hands along the well-loved walls like a blind person.

There was her parents' bedroom where she had a dim but certain memory of once walking in on their love-making and, next to it, Peter's room, his beloved collection of dinky cars no longer lined up, tail to bumper, on the pelmet. The kitchen was on her right and she could almost smell her mother's sweetly-spiced curries and mulberry cobblers so thick with syrup they would erupt into bright red streams when you broke the crust… like molten lava from a volcano, Peter used to say.

When she reached the lounge, its massive bay windows looking out onto the slate porch and, beyond it, the front lawn, she realised there was no-one else in the house. She tentatively called out but no-one replied. Opening the French door she stepped out onto the porch, and the smooth, sun-baked slate was warm under her feet. She sat down on the low brick wall which enclosed the slate and smiled, remembering the time when, desperate to cool down, they'd been allowed to use the hose pipe to fill the small outdoor enclosure of the porch with water.

Delighted with their very own swimming pool, she and Peter had wallowed and waded in the water, turned instantly warm by the hot slate beneath. They'd lain on their bellies and tried to doggy paddle in the one inch deep pool, kicking furiously as their knees grazed the stone.

It had ended all too quickly, the water trickling out through the cracks in the slate, and, before they knew it, they were lying on their stomachs in the empty porch like tiny beached whales.

Emma's mother had stood watching them from the French door, a dish towel in her hands. She'd looked so young and beautiful, her auburn hair turned to warm honey by the sun, her eyes deep blue and laughing.

Once they'd dried off she reappeared with a heaped plate of cinnamon toast and hot tea, which they ate sitting on the slate, letting it warm their icy bottoms.

That was the summer Harry started painting the garage. And

she gave an involuntarily shudder. In fact, now that she came to think of it, he'd been the one who'd dragged the heavy hose pipe from the back yard to the porch. It was all beginning to come back to her, clearer than she'd seen it in a long time.

Harry had been smiling shyly along with her mother while they swam and, when she'd come out with cinnamon toast and tea, she'd brought him some too.

He hadn't sat with them, but a respectable distance away, on a stone bench to one side of the porch.

Emma found herself once again wandering in her imagination over Harry's handsome features, his strong Roman nose, set in a long, chiselled face, skin the colour of milky coffee, hair, soft curls framing his head.

But it was his eyes, those thoughtful green pools, that got Emma every time. He was always so quiet, always in the background, but his eyes said so much more than words could express. When Emma looked into them she got the feeling she could go on looking forever. And again she felt the shudder, the cold fear of knowledge.

Harry sat that day drinking his tea, his big hands clumsily holding on to one of her mother's dainty china tea cups, trying his best not to spill. Every now and then he'd glance their way, his eyes lingering on Emma's mother just a little too long.

Of course these were only things she noticed now, looking back at them with adult eyes. Aged 10, all Emma had thought was that he was the most handsome man she'd ever seen.

Once Harry had finished his tea he excused himself to go back to his work, and Emma watched him leave.

Looking thoughtfully at him she asked her mother: "Mama, why does Harry talk funny?"

It wasn't said with malice so her mother patiently explained that there was nothing funny about the way he talked. He had a Coloured accent which was different to theirs, not funny.

"What's 'Coloured' Mama?"

"It's when someone had a Black Mom and a White Dad, or a White Mom and a Black Dad."

Her brows furrowed. "But how, Mama? Blacks aren't good enough to marry Whites."

She would never forget how her mother's gentle eyes flashed. "Emma Bridget Hardy, where on earth did you ever learn such a thing? You are never to talk like that again! Do you hear me?" And when Emma didn't reply, stunned into silence by her mother's uncharacteristic tone, her mother repeated, even louder: "Do you hear me?"

Emma could do little but nod her head, shocked tears pricking the back of her eyelids.

She was reminded of their conversation when, a little later, she started to notice how her mother talked to Harry, so different to the way her father did.

Emma's father was as loud as Harry was silent, as white as Harry was swarthy. You could hardly find two more contrasting men and, after reading a copy of Peter's *MAD* magazine, Emma had concluded they were a little like Spy versus Spy, one White, one Black, so different but somehow, in a way she couldn't quite fathom, there was something they shared.

When Emma's father arrived home from work each day, he'd be

11

calling Harry's name before he turned off the ignition.

"Harry! Harry! I need to see you! Harry, where are you, boy?" (Don't call him "boy" Emma's Mom would always say.)

Emma used to think Harry could have been Superman and still wouldn't have been able to get to her father's side in time for the second "Harry".

"Jah, Mr Hardy?"

"Harry, how's the painting coming along?" And before Harry could reply, "I've told you it has to be finished by the end of the week and it needs to be done properly, boy, none of this half-hearted slip-slop work you people are so good at. You got that?"

Harry wouldn't say a word throughout her father's loud remonstrations. Often, if her father was feeling particularly talkative, Harry could get away without having to say anything at all. Her father would ask and answer his own questions and, somehow, end matters feeling like he'd had a fully satisfying conversation.

Emma's Dad wasn't a hard man, he just liked to hide all his soft edges. At least that was how Peter had put it, sounding so worldly-wise, when Emma had cried to him that their father was "always so mean".

He'd grown up on a farm, helping his father raise cattle and harvest fields. He was small but wiry and, during his youth, had been a bit of a sports legend…and still had the calves and biceps to prove it.

When the family had fallen bankrupt after a series of droughts, the farm had been sold and they'd moved into the city.

With his easy, masculine ways and extrovert nature, it wasn't long before he found a job working as a salesman for a company dealing in "soft goods", which Emma thought seemed like a funny line of work for a man as strong as her father.

Some weekends Emma's Dad would invite his old school friends over with their families, and the men would braai while the women talked and laughed in the kitchen, preparing the salads and garlic bread and replenishing their husbands' beers.

Emma thought her Mom was the prettiest Mom there, and so did everyone else. She saw how people looked at her, the other Moms and Dads.

Sometimes on those evenings, and after a few beers, Emma's Dad would take her Mom's hand and pull her towards him. Once she saw him slap her Mom on the bottom. She tried to pull away, but Emma's Dad made it like a game, laughing low, and held her even tighter. Emma saw her Mom's face grow red.

During those family get-togethers Peter and Emma would be left to entertain the other children, a motley crew of snotty-nosed brats who bullied and brayed their way through the long, hot afternoons.

"Why don't you have a swimming pool?" said a nine-year old boy with blond hair almost the same shade as his skin and impossibly skinny legs that made his knees stand out like clenched fists. "My Dad says all White people have swimming pools. Blacks don't coz they can't swim. My Dad says it has something to do with their brains not being as big as ours."

"Well that's just stupid!" Emma countered, her mother's admonitions still fresh in her mind. But Peter, always the placid one, just rolled his eyes and ignored him.

Once, in a desperate bid to prove their social standing, Emma ignored Peter's sage advice and showed them the secret hideaway in the mulberry tree.

"We've got something much better than a swimming pool," Emma told the pair of fat, ruddy-cheeked twins she'd been saddled with for the afternoon.

"Jah, what?" they asked in unison.

"It's a magical, secret place," she said, eyes wide, waving her hands around like a magic wand, trying to make it sound every bit as fantastical as it was in her head.

"Hmmm, so where is it?" Some reluctant interest now.

"Well you first have to promise not to tell anyone or…" she fumbled, looking for a fitting punishment, "or…or I'll tell on you."

Before long the three of them were trekking through the scrubby thorn bushes which formed the back boundary to the yard, Emma at the head, holding a long stick to add an air of import to their expedition.

When they reached the mulberry tree she parted her arms like a game show hostess and proudly presented the object of their quest.

"That it?" scowled twin number one (their names, even back then, eluded her). "It's nothing but a tree!"

"Oh no, oh no, no no! It's much more than just a tree!" she

said shaking her head. "Come on, I'll show you!"

Nestled inside its leafy branches and even once she'd pointed out all the magical spots – the dappled leaves letting in golden flecks of sunlight, falling like glitter from the heavens; the home-made hammock where they would lie and dream for hours, the warm sun on their faces; the "castle turret", a particularly prominent branch in the centre – they were unimpressed.

"This is useless," grumbled twin number two, arms folded tightly across his chest. "But I guess if it's all you've got. Go get us something to drink and eat then it can be like a proper castle."

She rushed inside, rummaged through her mother's pantry and came racing back, excited and out of breath, carrying a packet of Marie biscuits and a bottle mixed with water and Mazoe orange.

As she ran up to the tree, the twins were on their way down.

"What happened?"

"We had enough but, hey, thanks, we'll take the grub," and they left.

A closer look at the tree and the puzzle was solved. The twins had pulled down the hammock and hacked away at branches and leaves. One had peed against the trunk.

When Peter came looking for her over an hour later she was still sitting up in the tree, her head on her knees, sobbing. They spent the next week restoring it to its former glory and, to his credit, Peter never once said "I told you so".

CHAPTER FOUR

EMMA WAS FAR away, lost in her thoughts, and the old woman had to call out to her twice before she heard her.

She leapt to her feet.

"Oh God, I'm so sorry! I woke up on the bed and I couldn't find anyone, I called out but…"

"Don't fret so," said the old woman, interrupting her. "You had a nasty fall, I thought I'd leave you to rest it off. Let's have a look at your arm."

"No it's fine, really, please don't worry!" But the old woman was already examining it through her wire-rimmed glasses, prodding it gently with her wrinkled fingertips.

"A little aloe and it'll be right as rain," she said, snapping off a leaf from a nearby plant and smearing its cold thick jelly on the graze.

"How are you feeling now?"

"A little disorientated, very embarrassed. I'm sorry for all the trouble I've caused you. With hindsight I realise I shouldn't have come."

"Nonsense! You can't keep ghosts down forever. Is that why you're here, Emma Groves?" she said, looking up at her. "Are you hunting ghosts?"

"It's complicated. So much has happened," said Emma, wrapping her arms around herself. "Yes, I guess I am. I really don't know anymore. I don't know much of anything."

"Well let's just simplify things a little, shall we?" said the old woman with a smile. "Do you know if you want a cup of tea? That I can help you with! Why don't you carry on sitting here, and I'll bring it out to you."

"Oh, you really don't have to do that. I don't want to be any more trouble..." Her protestations were cut short by a gentle hand on her arm and an assertive gesture towards a garden chair. Emma sat down and closed her eyes, pressing her fingertips to her throbbing temple.

Ten minutes later the old woman returned, a tray of tea and biscuits in her hands. She placed it on a table in front of Emma and sat down opposite her.

"I'm sorry, I've been so rude, I didn't even ask your name," said Emma.

"Elizabeth, dear, Elizabeth Calderwood."

"And how long have you lived here, if you don't mind my asking?"

"Must have been soon after you left. We bought it from the estate." The old woman looked down.

"Do you stay here alone?"

"Oh no. There's Jacob, the gardener, who let you in. He lives in the back and he carried you in when you took ill." Elizabeth was pouring tea from a large floral teapot into two white porcelain cups. "And Calvin who lives in the garage which we converted into an apartment. Of course since my husband died and the children left, it's just me in the main house," she said.

"Did your children grow up here?" asked Emma, taking one of the tea cups from her with a smile. "I have such great childhood memories, especially of the back yard, the mulberry tree. It was our special place, my brother and I."

"No, dear, my children were teenagers when we moved here, sadly done with making up games, more interested in going out with their friends. You look a lot like your mother," said Elizabeth, stirring sugar into her tea cup as she observed Emma. "I remember seeing pictures of her in the newspaper at the time. She was a beautiful woman."

Emma instinctively put her hand to her face, as if feeling her mother's high, distinctive cheek-bones, her small, slightly up-turned nose, velvet skin like rose petals, crushed so easily by the sun.

"Yes," she said, her voice catching, "she was. I don't think I look anything like her."

"That's because you're not looking closely enough."

Emma was starting to relax: this perfect summer afternoon, the familiar scent of sweet Persian jasmine in the air, the intensity of the sun diffusing as it slowly dipped towards the horizon.

"It's so incredible to be back here," said Emma, placing the delicate silver teaspoon on the table in front of her and lifting the tea cup. "I'd forgotten how beautiful it was. This kind of peace and tranquillity, you can't find it anywhere else in the world.

Which is ironic when you think of all the violence…" she trailed off.

"Do you have children?" asked Elizabeth.

"No," she said.

"You've come alone." It was a statement, not a question.

"My life isn't working out so well," said Emma, putting down her tea cup and dropping her eyes to her hands in her lap. "When I say life, I guess I mean marriage." She was startled by her own candour. "I needed to do this alone. I feel I've been doing it alone for so long anyway it doesn't really matter. Sometimes it feels like the last time I didn't feel alone was with Peter."

"Peter?"

"My brother, Peter." Dark shadows passed over her eyes.

Elizabeth sat back, her elbow resting on the arm of the chair, one finger lightly touching her thin lips. "You know, I think there's someone you should meet," she said. "Come with me!" She placed her hands on the arms of the garden chair and raised herself slowly up. Emma moved over to her to help but she waved her away.

She led Emma from the porch past the kitchen where a semi-curved outer wall had once shimmered with a colourful creeper lovingly tended by her mother. Today it was bare, varnished brick. They walked down the driveway where once, in the rainy season, Emma and Peter had dug for hours in the mud to build a city, carrying water in a pail from the tap to make a river that ran down to a long, curved dam wall. Their father came home to find them covered from head to toe in mud, and yelled to Harry to bring him the hose pipe so he could hose them down before sending them to their rooms.

They stopped at the garage – now an apartment, Emma remembered the old woman saying – and Elizabeth called out: "Calvin," and, when no-one replied, called out again, louder this time "Calvin! Calvin, where are you?"

A husky voice replied "Comin'" and, before long, a man rounded the corner from the back of the apartment and stood in front of them.

Emma's eyes widened. The smooth cappuccino-coloured skin, the piercing green eyes, the crown of soft curls.

"Oh my dear Lord…Harry!"

CHAPTER
FIVE

FOR THE SECOND TIME in one afternoon Emma felt like fainting.

Harry. Although, when the initial shock had subsided, an impossibly young Harry.

"Remember how I told you that ghosts don't stay down forever, Emma dear?" said Elizabeth, placing a hand gently on her arm. "I think the time has come to face yours. And I have a feeling you have more strength than you give yourself credit for. Emma, meet Calvin, Harry Rhoades' son."

Within minutes of their meeting, Emma was able to see that the similarities between father and son were only skin deep. Calvin was nothing at all like Harry. Like Harry he was incredibly good looking, tall and broad-chested with long legs and smooth skin pulled taut over clearly-defined muscles; unlike Harry he knew it.

But there was something else about Calvin, apart from his disturbing likeness to his father and all the troubling memories that went with him, a memory too deep in her sub-conscious to grasp.

He looked straight at Emma and she felt her cheeks grow warm.

"Calvin," said Elizabeth, interrupting his slow inspection. "This is…."

But before she could complete her sentence he said, quite softly, "Jah, I scheme I know who she is."

"Life has a funny way of coming full circle, my dear," said Elizabeth, gently grasping Emma's arm. "One day, about 10 years after we moved into this house, Calvin pitched up at our gate, scruffy and full of attitude – well at least more attitude than he has now, believe it or not," she said, smiling at him. "Like you, he was looking for answers that neither I nor this house could give him. It took 20 years for those answers to arrive, but arrive they did. You see, Calvin, I told you never to give up."

He didn't say a word.

With some difficulty, Elizabeth persuaded Emma to stay and eat with them, insisted she'd be offended if she didn't.

She disappeared into the kitchen to put the finishing touches to the dinner, refusing any help and instructing Calvin to entertain Emma on the porch. Calvin was sitting across from her and staring, his body leaning forward, elbows resting on his knees and fingers interlaced under his chin.

She was having trouble reading his look.

"This is my first time back in 30 years and, in a funny way, it's hardly changed." She was nervous, trying hard to break the icy silence.

No reaction.

"My brother and I used to play in the mulberry tree behind your apartment."

At last a reaction; the smallest tightening at the corner of his mouth.

"Your bro, the faggot," his accent so like Harry's.

"What did you say?"

"I tuned, I knows wat ya bro is," he drawled.

Somewhere through her fiery anger, an image: Peter, always the peacemaker, Emma the feisty one, urging him to retaliate, small and plump but willing to fight his battles if she had to.

Her first instinct was to leap over the table separating them and grab Calvin by the throat as she would have done once when some bully in the playground made fun of her beloved brother.

She flung her chair back and leapt to her feet. Just then Elizabeth emerged from the kitchen and, coolly taking in the scene, laughed softly and shook her head.

"Two minutes, Calvin, that's all it took for you to be outrageously rude, wasn't it?" She placed a steaming casserole dish on the table. "I thought you might have just a little respect for our guest and behave for, maybe, five? Emma, my dear, he's an angry, immature child", she said, taking off her oven gloves and placing them on the table and, when he protested, "yes, Calvin, that's exactly what you are and you know it!" Then she looked directly at Emma and said, "Try, as hard as you can, Emma, not to take anything he says to heart; there is as much pain in him as there is in you. Whether you like it or not you're twinned by sadness. And when you both realise that, you'll get on just fine. Now Calvin, go get us some drinks, maybe that way – though I can't guarantee it – you'll stay out of trouble."

Calvin spent the rest of the evening drinking himself into an angry stupor. In spite of what Elizabeth had said, Emma still wanted nothing to do with him.

The two women made small talk; they had had enough drama for one day. By the time the full moon, butter yellow on the horizon, had started to rise, Emma thanked Elizabeth for the dinner, telling her it was time she was off.

"Come, come dear, it's still early and where will you stay?"

She had planned to check into the local Holiday Inn, if it was still standing after all this time.

"Why don't you stay here? You're most welcome. This is, after all, your home."

"WAS her home," slurred Calvin from the shadows. He was leaning back against the wall, his arms folded over his chest, his long legs stretched out in front of him, one ankle crossed over the other.

"I don't want to make things awkward," she said, glancing at him, "I think it's best I go."

"Don't pay him any attention," said Elizabeth, rising out of her chair and walking towards her.

"Thank you, but I really think it would be best I check into a hotel. If you don't mind, I'd really like to come back tomorrow during the day and take some photographs."

"Of course I don't mind," said Elizabeth, grasping her hand in hers. "You come back any time you please. I'm in all day."

Emma impulsively bent to hug the old woman, feeling her sharp bones through her shoulders.

Nodding vaguely in Calvin's direction she gathered together her things, stepped into her hired car and drove off.

The Holiday Inn was still there and Emma booked into a clean but impersonal room overlooking the swimming pool. She couldn't take the airlessness and stepped out onto the small balcony to breathe in the cool night air. There had been a bit of work done to the gardens and playground but, otherwise, it was almost exactly as she remembered.

She thought back to sweltering Sundays when the family would come to the hotel for lunch, she and Peter swimming for hours in the pool, always icy cold in the brooding shadow of the hotel building; running up the massive slide in the playground and rocketing down the other side. Swinging side-by-side, seeing whose feet could reach the highest, shrieking with the thrill of feeling like they were going to turn upside down.

Her father had seemed happy then, his ever-present beer in one hand, wife in the other.

She closed her eyes and saw once again her father lean in close to her mother, whisper something in her ear, and her mother turn her head away, shrugging her shoulders.

A waiter – Black, of course – walked towards them with drinks and, once again, the startling contrast between her mother and her father. Without even looking at him, his eyes still locked on his wife, her father gestured impatiently for him to set the tray down on the table. Her mother looked at the man with a mixture of apology and kindness, but her father placed his hand under her chin and turned her face back to his. The waiter bowed slightly and walked away.

CHAPTER
SIX

EMMA SPENT A restless night tossing and turning on the stiff hotel mattress, starched sheets holding her like chains. She was haunted by memories that flashed in front of her, mingling into a frightening collage, and was relieved when morning finally came.

Calculating the time difference she thought she'd better call Daniel; she'd had no contact with him since she flew out of the States three days ago.

It would be 11pm and she imagined him still sitting in front of his computer, a spot he occupied almost from the moment he arrived home from work around 7 until way into the early hours of the morning, long after Emma had gone to bed.

She still needed to organise a local sim card for her phone, so she booked the call through reception and, after about 10 minutes, the hotel phone rang.

"I'm sorry ma'am, I'm getting no reply from the call you placed."

"Are you sure? Could you try again?" She was sitting on the edge of the bed, cradling the phone between her ear and her raised shoulder as she rubbed cream into her hands.

"I tried three times ma'am – no reply – but I'll continue trying if you wish."

"Please, if you could."

She put down the phone and carried on rubbing her hands together. Daniel was out? Unlikely. Or sleeping so deeply he didn't hear the phone ring? Even more unlikely. He was a light sleeper.

After several more failed attempts, Emma decided to call his cell from her phone, even though she knew the charges would be astronomical. This time success after the first try.

Daniel's voice was familiar yet different, possibly just the long distance. No, something else: an edge to it.

"Hey, how's it going?"

"Good, good. You? How's Africa?" and he pronounced it with a long mocking "A".

"Um, interesting. Too much to say on the phone." Too much to say in person either. "Where are you? I called the house." She was pacing the room.

"Oh that, oh, right… just out on a work thing, you know…."

No, she didn't know. Daniel never went out on 'work things'.

"Where?" Somehow she couldn't edge out the jealousy she could hear creeping into her voice, hypocritical as it seemed.

"Palermo's." One of her favourite restaurants. Not much of a venue for a work do.

"Palermo's?" She stopped pacing. "Good, enjoy. Say hi to Giovanni for me."

"Who?"

"Say hi to Giovanni, the maître d'…"

27

"Oh, Giovanni, yes of course Giovanni, yes, yes, I will."

"I just wanted to let you know I arrived safely. All is well."

"OK, where you staying?"

"I booked into the local Holiday Inn."

"Good, good."

A pause.

"I'll call again in a couple of days, once I know my plans," she said.

"Yes, yes, do that. Good. Well you take care now."

You take care now? She got a "you take care now" like the woman behind the car rental counter? What the hell!

But all she said was "You too", and hung up. And she realised as she put down the phone that her hands were shaking.

She was confused by Daniel's behaviour but more by her own. Had he found out? No, how could he have? She'd been meticulously careful, left no clues. She double-checked her luggage and, sure enough, her lap-top was there.

This was just how Daniel would react if he did find out, act like nothing had happened. Avoid the whole issue, pretend everything was fine. And suddenly, somehow, she found herself wishing he had found out, wishing he would rage and rant and scream, care enough to confront her about it. Then it would be out in the open and she wouldn't have to keep the lid so tightly closed on her guilt it threatened to heat up inside her, reach boiling point and bubble over.

She couldn't bear to be alone any longer. She called down to reception and found out they had no Wi-Fi in the rooms but that there was an internet café on the ground floor. She rushed downstairs, connected to Skype and looked for Alan. When she saw he was signed-in, she almost cried with relief.

CHAPTER
SEVEN

EMMA PULLED UP at the gate of number 17 and waited for the gardener to unlock it for her. The grey granite wall had a distinctive shadow showing where it had been raised by her father during the war. A low, neighbourly wall was no longer the thing; you needed something tall and imposing to keep out the evil. As long as the evil was on the outside in the first place. Harry's image flashed in front of her again.

Elizabeth looked up from a bed of lavender she was inspecting when she heard the car pull into the yard.

She straightened up slowly and waved a warm greeting, shuffling towards the car.

"Oh my dear, I'm so glad you came back!" said Elizabeth as Emma stepped out of the car, taking both her hands in hers and smiling warmly at her. "I was worried that after Calvin's appalling little performance last night you'd be scared off for good."

"Pity for Calvin it takes more than that to scare me," she said, smiling.

"You know I'm just a scatty-brained old woman and you must

forgive me," she said, tapping her forehead lightly with two fingers. "Only after you'd left I remembered there was a box of things that belonged to your family. I remember my husband enquiring at the time whom he should send them on to, but with you all so far away, no-one could tell us. We just kept it in the storeroom, not knowing what else to do with it. Luckily for you I'm a squirrel, never throw a darn thing away, so it's still there. Come, come, I'll show you!"

She took Emma's hand and breathlessly led her to the storeroom. Elizabeth had been right when she called herself a squirrel: the small two by four metre room was packed almost to the ceiling with boxes, broken bicycle frames, half-finished projects, tools, and all sorts of rubbish. When she flung open the door, the dust displaced by the incoming air flew up and glittered in the sunlight coming through from the small, square window near the ceiling.

"It might be a little hard to get to it. Calvin? Calvin, I need you!" And, seeing Emma tense, she put a hand on her arm and laughed softly, "Don't you worry about him, he'll be nursing a hangover so big just opening his eyes is going to hurt. He won't be giving you any trouble."

Calvin shuffled around from the back of the apartment, hand shielding his bloodshot eyes from the glare.

She nodded in his direction and he grunted, before disappearing into the store room and eventually emerging with a giant box on one shoulder.

He threw it to the ground, grunted loudly and disappeared again.

"Thank you dear," called Elizabeth after him and, winking mischievously at Emma, whispered, "You see, I told you he'd be as quiet as a lamb."

Emma sat cross-legged on the floor under the shady overhang of the store room roof, the dusty box in front of her. Elizabeth excused herself, disappearing into the house, and Emma was left alone.

She didn't open the box immediately, caught up between conflicting emotions of excitement and fear.

Slowly she lifted one flap and then the other and tentatively pressed them back. Years in storage had taken its toll on the contents: everything was covered in a thick film of dust and there was evidence of rats.

At the very top of the box was an enlarged photograph in a gilt frame which Emma immediately recognised as her parents' wedding picture.

She dusted away several layers of grime to look again into the youthful, loving eyes of her mother and father, an image that had looked down at her from the mantelpiece in the lounge her entire childhood. What struck her now was how the light in their eyes had faded over the years, like a battery-powered light, so powerful at first, slowly dimming as the power ran out.

The last picture she had of them in her mind, the light had faded to a dull yellow speck, barely alive at all.

Haunted, she quickly put the photograph to one side and kept digging.

The box turned out to be a treasure chest of photographs, ornaments, greeting cards and keepsakes, each bringing with it a vivid memory, sometimes so intense it burnt deep in her chest.

There was a whole pile of birthday and Christmas cards which her mother had held on to with the hope of one day putting them into a scrap book. Cards congratulating her parents on Peter's birth and, two years later, hers, cards from friends and family for every birthday, cards from almost every Christmas since they were married.

In the early days her parents had always made a special point of celebrating their wedding anniversary and the cards they sent to each other were tied together with a lavender ribbon. Unlike everything else which had been tossed into the box, someone had taken extra care with these.

She untied the ribbon and put it to one side and started to go through the cards, feeling somehow an intruder. They were her parents but their love for each other was a realm she never entered, probably because, considering all that had happened, she found it so hard to understand.

Each card was a declaration of deep, undying love, her mother's perhaps more poetic and eloquent, but her father's, in their simplicity and raw emotion, probably even more stirring.

She couldn't believe these were the words of the man she knew; she had never seen a side of him so vulnerable and full of feeling. Gone was the brashness, the ego, the impenetrably tough facade; what was left was pure, unconditional, if not slightly obsessive, love.

It felt too intimate for anyone other than the couple to be reading, like that time she'd walked into her parents' room when they were making love. She was too young to recognise the heaving sounds of passion or understand her father's slurred entreaties to her mother: "Don't stop! Never, never stop!"

Neither did she understand why her mother, when she realised Emma was in the room and sat up, startled, wasn't wearing any clothes. She pulled the sheet up to her chin and told Emma gently but firmly to go back to her room; there was an odd thickness to her voice. She followed a few minutes later, clutching her gown tightly to her chest with one hand.

When she sat on the edge of the bed and soothed Emma's brow, damp with fever, the little girl looked closely at her mother and saw two bright spots on her cheeks she'd never noticed before.

"Mama, why weren't you wearing any clothes?"

"Oh honey, it's so hot, I just took off my nightie for a moment to cool down a little."

"Can I take my nightie off too? I'm also hot."

"No, love, you can't. You're hot because you have a fever, you must keep your nightie on, OK?"

She waited with Emma a little while, then kissed her lightly on the forehead and quietly left the room.

Emma felt suddenly sad that her mother had never been able to tell her the real reason she was naked, that they'd never had a chance to sit and talk about love and passion and sex. She'd had to fumble through it alone, not having a clue about any of it and no-one to talk to.

She closed her eyes, thinking about the mistakes she might have prevented along the way, how her relationships with men might have been different if she hadn't been entering every sexual encounter like a student sitting an exam without having the slightest clue about the coursework.

With hindsight she had pretty much fumbled her way from one relationship to another, somehow ending up in the biggest fumble of all: her marriage.

At the beginning Daniel had been quite gentle and understanding about her clumsy sexuality and inexperience.

But he hadn't anticipated her inhibitions or realised just how deeply her insecurities and fears ran. In all fairness he gave it his best shot but, somehow, just didn't have what she needed to unlock the passions so deep inside her she didn't know they existed.

Their sex life dwindled, then died altogether.

It had taken another man to help her find the key – and once the floodgates were opened they were almost impossible to control.

Her mind drifted back to Alan, to the guilt and the ecstasy, the pain and remorse, the passion, once ignited, that she had no idea how to extinguish, hard as she tried. She closed her eyes.

When she opened them she saw a curtain in the apartment flutter.

CHAPTER
EIGHT

BY THE TIME Emma had finished going through the contents of the box she felt completely drained.

Perhaps her most difficult find had been the jewellery box Peter had given her for her ninth birthday. It was small and round, purple satin with the delicate figurine of an angel on the top. When she'd torn off the wrapping paper she'd shrieked with delight and then opened the box to find a pair of dainty gold studs.

"Earrings! Mama, Daddy, earrings!" she shouted out, clasping Peter round the neck and bobbing excitedly up and down.

Her father looked on stonily before turning to her mother and saying in an angry whisper: "Who gave him permission to buy her earrings?"

Her mother kept the smile frozen on her face and, through clenched teeth, whispered back, "We can talk about this later."

Her father set his chin. "We will talk about it now. I've made my feelings very clear, yet you continually conspire behind my back."

Still smiling stiffly she turned to the children and said with forced cheer: "Come on you two, enough jumping about, there's cake in the kitchen; go make the tea and bring it on to the porch."

A little confused but too excited to let it dampen their spirits, Emma and Peter ran to the kitchen and, as they left, heard their parents' tense voices.

That was the day Emma had called her father mean, and Peter, despite the fact that his gift, bought, in part, with his pocket money, was the subject of the argument, tried to defend him.

"He just hides all his soft edges."

Emma thought back to the stack of anniversary cards and realised there was probably only one time he did show his soft edges, bare and exposed.

In the end Emma decided to keep only the cards, the wedding photo and the jewellery box; the rest she threw away. She bundled them all into a packet and then headed to the kitchen in search of Elizabeth.

She found her working in the sunlit kitchen, washing and chopping a stack of vegetables freshly-picked from the garden.

"Hello dear," she said, turning around when she heard Emma's footsteps at the door. Then wiping her hands with a dish towel she walked over and looked closely at her. "You look all worn-out; I think a hot cup of tea is in order."

Emma smiled her thanks. "God, you must think I'm such a basket case! I'm not always like this you know."

"It's not every day we face the ghosts of our childhood, my dear," said Elizabeth, filling a red plastic jug with water from the tap and pouring it into the kettle. "This can't be easy for you. If the newspaper reports are to be believed, you saw and knew more about the ugliness of the world than any little girl ought to. How did you cope?" The old woman turned to look at her and her eyes were kind and understanding.

"I don't think I coped at all, Elizabeth. That's why I'm at this point in my life. Forty two years old and not sure what it's about, not any of it," said Emma, standing with her back against the kitchen counter and resting one elbow on it.

"Not sure if any of us really do, my dear, and that's the sad truth." She pulled two mugs from a cupboard overhead. "Take Calvin, for example, the most promising young man I know, talented in so many ways. A different time, a different place, certainly if he'd been dealt a better hand in family, upbringing, he could have made something of his life. Instead he's basically a 35 year old gigolo – and don't laugh, it's the truth! – who believes he'll find the answers in sex and alcohol, or damn well die trying!"

"What made you take him in?" asked Emma.

"It's a funny thing, dear," she paused as she took two tea bags from a glass canister and dropped them into a teapot. "He looked so pitiful, so broken up, searching for something. My husband and I had followed the case very closely in the papers at the time. I hope it's not too hard for you to hear this, considering how deeply it affected your family, but we saw Harry as a tragic victim of circumstance, just like you all were."

Emma nodded slightly, unable to separate the loss of her family with her feelings about Harry.

"Besides, we needed a handy man. It was just good timing I guess." She emptied the boiling water from the kettle into the teapot, steam rising and misting over her glasses. "I certainly never imagined he'd still be with us 20 years later. He just kind of grew on us. I see you look surprised," she said looking over at Emma. "You don't know him well enough. Just give him a chance and you'll see: he has a way of getting under your skin." And her eyes were bright.

"Speak of the devil and the devil is sure to appear," said Elizabeth clapping her hands lightly together as Calvin hulked in the doorway. "Look who's finally up! Good evening dear, how are you feeling? Well from the grunt I'll assume you're still alive so that's good news at least! Can you manage some food? It'll make you feel better."

Emma marvelled at the old woman's patience and watched as she slowly but expertly coerced the sulking Calvin into a better mood, cooking him a massive plate of egg and toast followed by a mug of strong, percolated black coffee the size of a small soup bowl.

By the end of it Calvin looked almost human again.

Every now and then Emma would steal a quick glance in his direction, still something about him prodding insistently at her memory, just beyond her grasp, and beginning to trouble her more and more.

"So, my dear," said Elizabeth, folding her hands on the table in front of her and sounding suddenly business-like, "I've been thinking and, yes, Calvin, you know how dangerous that can be! I've been thinking about you staying all the way off in a cold hotel room while I have this empty house just standing here. Why not just check out of that place and come stay with us?"

"Oh Lord, I've caused you so much inconvenience already!" said Emma, "I'd feel terrible imposing myself on you even more."

"Nonsense, my dear! We'd love to have you," she said, reaching over and stroking her arm.

"If you're really certain it's OK with you, that would be wonderful. Thank you so much."

"Oh, I'm so pleased," said Elizabeth, clasping her hands together under her chin.

"I don't intend to stay long – a few days, tops."

"You stay just as long as you want, as long as you need to. My home is your home…well, it literally is!" and she laughed at her own quip. "My one rule is no standing on ceremony. I want you to come and go as you please, and I'll do the same. And, to prove it, I've a lot to get on with, so I'll excuse myself and let you get on with whatever it is you need to do. Dinner at seven OK with you?"

Pulling out of the driveway on her way to the hotel to pack up her things and check out, Elizabeth's bony bent figure waving farewell, Emma had the oddest feeling. It was a feeling so foreign she almost didn't recognise it, the warm, old familiar glow that started in her chest and spread right through her. She'd forgotten what being home felt like.

That night she lay in her old room listening to the sounds of a storm rattling and raging around the little house. The build-up of thunder followed by a moment of utter silence before the rain started falling, gently at first then steadily rising in sound and intensity until it was pounding the iron roof, drowning out every other noise.

At the peak of the storm she stepped out of bed and walked to the window, watching the curtain of water plummet to the ground and run in rivers to the back of the yard. She sucked in deep breaths of the glorious smell of rain seeping through dry earth, a smell like none other she had ever smelt, one, if she could only bottle it, she would have soaked herself in all those long, lonely years away from here.

It was storming so hard it was difficult to see further than a couple of metres in front of her but, beyond the sheet of rain, she thought she saw a flutter of colour. What looked like a figure standing in the middle of the storm, arms raised to the heavens, face uplifted so the rain would have battered his face. It was Calvin, it could only be him. There was something about the way he was standing there that made her think of a Baptism.

Finally, the figure walked back towards the apartment. Emma went back to bed but couldn't sleep, lying there for hours, thinking about Calvin in the rain, wondering if he had been able to find the redemption she'd been searching for her whole life.

CHAPTER NINE

THE NEXT MORNING the sun was out, making the glistening drops of rain still clinging to the tall grass stalks shimmer, and turning the garden into a bright, newly-washed wonderland. Emma looked out of her bedroom window and smiled. Elizabeth greeted her warmly in the kitchen, happy for her company, and Calvin, who walked in looking for breakfast soon afterwards, was fully-recovered and seemed in a better mood. He had a series of projects lined up.

He did contract work around the neighbourhood, much like Harry had done, and earned his keep at number 17 by doing work for Elizabeth wherever and whenever she needed. They didn't say it but with the crime rate rising he also provided much-needed security for the old woman.

Like his father he could turn his hand to almost anything, from fixing a car to laying electrical cable to building an extension.

"He's just amazing," Elizabeth told Emma with distinctive pride in her voice. They were standing side-by-side at the kitchen sink doing the breakfast dishes. "Once he puts his mind to it, there's nothing he can't do. And if he doesn't initially know how to do it, he'll work at it until he does. He never gives up. So it always surprises me how easily he gives up on himself."

"What do you know about his background?"

"Well, obviously I didn't know Harry personally, only what I read about in the newspaper following the accident." She was removing the dishes one-by-one from the sink and handing them to Emma to dry. "As for the rest of his family, the age-old story I'm afraid, perpetuating the stereotypes I so hate: his mother's an alcoholic, been married twice, shacked up with goodness knows how many men. Two sisters, beautiful girls with tragic circumstances. I've come to know the younger one, Talia, quite well. She sometimes comes around to visit Calvin.

"Both sisters live in the tiny family apartment with their mother, three children between them." She took the dried teapot and mugs from Emma's hands and put them away in the overhead cupboard. "Calvin's the only one in the family working. He doesn't talk about them much, but religiously visits every month and gives them money. What little he has – and hasn't blown on wine, women and song!" Elizabeth stood up, rested her back against the counter and crossed her arms on her chest.

"They live in a squalid apartment block in the bad end of town, run-down and neglected like all the homes Calvin ever had growing up."

Emma's mind ran reluctantly back to one of Calvin's childhood homes, the only one she'd seen, the one she'd never forget. That nagging memory again, why wouldn't it stay long enough for her to hold?

She was jolted back to reality by Elizabeth's voice. "So that's Calvin's sad tale. Not very different to all the other stories told by the residents of Somerset or Sunnyside or any of the other suburbs like it." She put the last of the dishes away then sat down at the kitchen table, slightly out of breath.

"What Calvin had over those still living there was the insight to get out before it was too late. One thing I've learnt in life is you can't judge a person by his background. Everyone deserves a second chance."

Emma looked out of the kitchen window and saw Calvin absorbed in the task of measuring the driveway, the plan being to pave it with keystone blocks before the rainy season set in. Last night's storm had reminded him he didn't have much time.

His muscles pressed through his thin cotton vest as he bent down, determined in his task with, she imagined, thoughts of anything else tucked safely away for now.

A second chance? What she wouldn't have done for a second chance herself – for them all. If only she could go back and rewrite their history, if only she could shrug off her own culpability.

The question was, how far would she have to go back in order to re-tell their story? Surely they had all been flawed, floundering from the very beginning. Would she have to start at the point where her father met her mother or go back even further than that?

And what guarantee was there that, even if things were different, they wouldn't still have found themselves treading the same destructive path, barrelling uncontrollably towards the series of events which would end so many lives, of both the living and the dead.

Right after it happened, the children had been sent to stay with their father's aunt, a grim, humourless spinster they were instructed to call Granny Mavis. A week later, arrangements were made for them to fly to Seattle where they were to live with their mother's only sister, Leigh.

The first month at least was a complete blur. Emma didn't remember saying goodbye to anyone, although she was sure there had been some kind of farewell before they were bundled, stunned and confused, onto the plane. Their first time on a plane should have been exciting but, for Emma, it remained one of her most frightening memories of a terrifying time. The only saving grace was having Peter there with her, but it wasn't the Peter she knew. It was a deathly quiet Peter who hardly spoke, who barely looked at her at all.

The air hostesses had been kind and understanding but it didn't help to ease the pain and bewilderment of being plucked from everything they knew and flung into the unknown.

Aunt Leigh was at the airport to meet them and as soon as she saw them grasped them both in her arms at once and sobbed uncontrollably, repeating over and over, "My babies, my poor, poor babies". Emma remembered being too stunned to cry.

Aunt Leigh, so like their mother in looks but nothing else, took them to her second floor apartment in the University District and showed them to their tiny little room, looking out onto the busy high street below. The first few nights they were hardly able to sleep at all, the noise from the traffic was so loud.

And when the phone rang through the thin walls from the next-door apartment, it sounded so close Emma was sure it was ringing right there in the room.

Their aunt tried her best to provide them with the comfort and support they needed, but she had never had children of her own, was a career student who was currently on her third degree, and was dealing with issues so far out of her realm of experience it was like the blind leading the blind.

She glanced out of the window again at Calvin and wondered what the first few months had been like for him, if there had been someone there, trying to comfort him through the pain.

CHAPTER
TEN

EMMA HAD OFFERED to cook dinner that night and once she'd cut the lamb up into bite size chunks and set them to simmer with onion, garlic and ginger, she walked outside into the sunshine where Calvin was still busy working.

At first he was so absorbed in his task he didn't notice her. Finally she had to cough slightly to let him know she was there. He glanced up, but only for a second before bending his head back down to his tape measure.

"Were you also having trouble sleeping last night?" she ventured as a way of starting up a conversation.

"Huh?"

"Last night, during the storm, I couldn't sleep either. I saw you outside."

"Uh-huh."

"What exactly were you doing out there?"

"Nothin'."

"Weren't you scared of the lightning?"

"D'ya always hafta aks a span of questions?"

"No, I'm also quite good at answering them, but someone has to ask me one first."

"Lekker. Well I'll tune you one: do you wanna make yourself useful?"

"What do you mean?"

"Wat I'm tuning, is, d'ya wanna stand round praating all day or do'ya wanna graft?"

"No, I mean what do you mean by lekker?"

"Good, cool, fine, wateva."

"And praating?"

"Talking, yacking, you know, like you women smaak – like – to do."

"Well I…" Before she could say any more he'd thrust the tape measure into her hand and, grabbing one end, started pulling it slowly out the width of the driveway, instructing her to stand where she was.

"Jus' anchor there, that's all ya gotta do. No praating required. Scheme ya can handle that?"

"Yeah, sure I can handle it, it's just that…" again he cut her off, this time with a finger to his lips, so she stopped.

In complete silence, following his hand signals, they quickly developed a routine, working together to measure the width and length of the drive, all the way from the gate to the apartment, with Calvin jotting down the measurements on the back of a manila envelope tucked under his chin. It would have taken a lot longer to do it alone but, when they were done, Calvin hardly acknowledged her help at all.

"You're welcome," she said when he indicated, again with

nothing but an abrupt hand signal, that they were done.

He looked up, puzzled, his face set until then in determined concentration. "Huh? Oh, jah. Thanks. Ya'll do."

She couldn't help but smile and, shaking her head, made to walk back into the house to check on the dinner.

"Like tears from the heavens," his voice, suddenly uncharacteristically soft, halted her in her tracks.

"Sorry?" She turned back.

"That's wat my o' bali used to say 'bout the rain: like tears from the heavens. I scheme if anyone'd know 'bout tears, be my o' bali."

Emma wanted to say something but was lost for words. Besides, Calvin had gone right back to his work as if, like before, she didn't exist at all.

Perplexed, and feeling sad all over again, she went back to the kitchen and carried on preparing the stew.

At dinner that evening Calvin had actually made an effort. He was freshly-shaven, emphasising the strong, clean lines of his face, and had changed into smart jeans and a polo shirt.

After finishing cooking, Emma showered and washed her hair, aware of the way the smell of cooking spices lingered in it, and, on impulse, put on the one nice outfit she had brought along with her: a long-length saffron Indian cotton dress, dotted with sequins, which followed the lines of her curves without exaggerating them.

When she stepped onto the porch where the table was laid, Calvin glanced up and then took a second look.

"Why Emma, dear, you look beautiful and, my, doesn't that smell gorgeous!" said Elizabeth inhaling the steam from the stew and the aromatic rice beside it.

"Thanks. I hope you enjoy it," she said, setting the dishes down on the table and taking a seat.

The rains of the night before had left everything fragrantly-fresh and newly-washed and it turned out to be one of the most pleasant evenings Emma could remember having in a long time.

Elizabeth and Emma did most of the talking and although Calvin hardly contributed at all, he was clearly listening.

Soon after dinner he scraped back his chair and announced that he was off.

"Off where, dear? Although, goodness knows, you're old enough to do as you wish," said Elizabeth, gathering together the dinner plates and piling them on top of each other. "I just thought you might stay and keep Emma and me company. Aren't there things you want to ask Emma, questions about the past? I think it's time we stopped pretending there's nothing weightier to talk about than how to make lamb stew."

"I gotta date. And there's nothin' she can tell me I don't already know." And with that he grabbed his jacket and stormed up the dark driveway.

The two women watched him leave.

"After all these years it still hurts so badly when you scratch just below the surface," said Elizabeth turning to look at Emma. "But then I don't need to tell you that, dear, do I?"

CHAPTER
ELEVEN

THAT NIGHT EMMA dreamt of Alan. She woke up flushed, her body still tingling with desire, the ache of disappointment intense.

She lay there for a long time, her night gown rising and falling with her ragged breath.

Like so much in her life, Alan never should have happened.

Two years ago she and Daniel had been invited to the 40th birthday party of one of her old college friends.

"Listen to this," said Emma walking towards him as he sat eating breakfast, the invitation in her hand, "we're invited to Stacey's 40th, in Miami of all places! How about that?"

"How about it?" he said without raising his head from the newspaper, laid out on the table beside his cereal bowl.

"Well don't you want to go?"

"To the 40th birthday party of someone I hardly know in a city I despise?" he glanced up, intense brown eyes hooded under a mop of thick black hair. "No, Emma, I don't."

"Well I do," she said, feeling every bit the spoilt child she was beginning to sound.

"Well you go then."

"Alone?"

"Why not?"

"You wouldn't mind?"

"Mind? Why ever would I mind?" A shadow of a smile around his hard mouth. "Who knows? Maybe you'll meet some hunky Latino who'll light your fire." Coming from anyone else it might have sounded frivolous, but on Daniel's lips it was cruel.

Emma called Stacey and told her she'd be arriving on the 2pm flight the Friday before the party, heading back on Sunday evening. Thankfully she didn't ask for details when Emma told her she'd be coming alone.

Boarding the flight that balmy August morning, Emma realised it was the first time she'd been anywhere without Daniel in almost eight years. The feeling was both frightening and intoxicating.

The minute she landed in Miami she felt like a new woman. Stacey was there to meet her and told her how great she was looking. Emma knew she'd put on weight and her face was looking tired and drawn, but was grateful for her friend's lie. Besides, when she looked at herself in the bathroom mirror in the elegant hotel room Stacey had booked her into, she was pleasantly surprised to see how much better she was looking already.

She hadn't seen her friend in over five years. Stacey was newly-divorced and on what seemed like a personal mission to sleep with every available man in Miami.

"I'm sowing my wild oats all over again!" she said, throwing back her head and tossing her long black sheen of hair. "I'd forgotten how much fun it was being single. Should never have married the old bore in the first place!"

The current man in her life was 15 years younger than her, an ex-football player in a minor league team. A knee injury had cut short his career and he'd turned to modelling. He and Stacey had met at the after-party of one of his shows.

"Course I know why he's with me, but what the hell! I'm having fun, he's having fun; we both know it won't last forever. God, who would want it to?" She'd pulled a compact from her bag and peered into it while she ran a manicured middle finger under each eye to blend in any stray traces of eye liner. "And the sex is fantastic! Don't look so horrified, babe," she said glancing at Emma over the compact. "We're 40, we're allowed to say the word 'sex'." Then she snapped the mirror shut, slapped it determinedly down on the table in front of her and said, "There, I said it again: sex, sex, sex, sex!"

"I think we get the message, Stace," said Emma with a laugh, reaching out and touching her friend lightly on the arm. "You're making the other diners jealous."

They had talked and laughed long after the last diners had left the restaurant, both having drunk too much wine.

Emma found herself telling her friend about the dismal state of her marriage, the first person she'd confided in besides her therapist.

"Fucking shrinks," said Emma, holding her wine glass lightly between her fingers and swirling the burgundy contents at the bottom, watching as the flecks of light reflected from the chandelier overhead bobbed and danced in it. "Always going on about how we marry men like our fathers, end up like our mothers. Daniel's nothing like my father, he's never given a shit about me. My father – now my father – there was a man who loved his wife. Loved her to death!"

"What'ya mean?" Stacey was hunched over her glass, bleary eyed.

"You know, loved her till there was nothing left. Nothing, nothing..." Unbearable sorrow began to break through the drunken haze. Before she knew it she was crying, loud, gasping drunken tears and Stacey was crying along with her, although she wasn't sure why.

Eventually the waiter was forced to tactfully tell them the restaurant was closing and offer his assistance to help them to their cars.

"Ooh, I wouldn't mind a little help from you, you look like you know how to help a woman," said Stacey and winked at the young waiter before being dragged off by Emma.

"We'll be fine, thank you," she said, trying her best not to slur.

The next day Emma had the worst headache of her life and couldn't remember half of what she'd said.

She had a vague recollection when the same young waiter came to take her breakfast order, giving her a knowing smile.

She ordered strong, black coffee and kept her sunglasses on.

Stacey, hardened by a regular diet of drinking and partying, was in much better shape when she picked Emma up at nine.

There were party preparations to finalise and Stacey wanted to give Emma the grand Miami tour. She spent the day feeling like an heiress, shopping at chrome-and-glass designer shops where Stacey was obviously a regular customer, being served complimentary glasses of wine – which Emma couldn't face but Stacey threw back with ease – eating lunch at a seafood restaurant overlooking the harbour and driving past the marina to see the yachts of the rich and famous.

Tom joined them for lunch, pulled his chair up close to Stacey and sat throughout the lunch with his hand on her thigh. He didn't say much but, as Stacey laughingly commented afterwards, who needed conversational skills with a butt like that?

At Stacey's insistence, Emma splurged on a black cocktail dress; it was short and revealing and far too expensive, nothing close to the sensible skirt and blouse she'd packed for the party, but she was feeling uncharacteristically impulsive.

When she slipped into it in her hotel room that evening she looked into the mirror and, for the first time in a long while, liked what she saw.

Her cheeks were flushed and healthy-looking, her eyes were unusually clear and bright, her hair was doing what it did on the rare occasions when it co-operated, falling softly to her shoulders, a natural healthy sheen running through it like golden highlights.

She stepped back, satisfied, grabbed her purse and ran downstairs to meet Stacey.

Initially she felt a little lost, missing the companionship of a partner at a social occasion, if not the partner himself.

Stacey had put her at a table made up of her closest friends, with rushed instructions that they take care of her, before flitting off to socialise with her other guests.

Alan was one of the guests at the table, introduced to her as Alan Graham, Stacey's accountant and alone at the party because he and his wife had had a fight before leaving for the party and she'd refused to come. He was a pleasant-enough looking man, sandy brown hair, a goatee, average height with just the slightest hint of a beer belly. He wore round glasses and his eyes, even behind glass, were his most striking feature: greyish-blue and with a brightness in them that lit up his face.

"God, I just wish women would come out and say what they want instead of expecting us to be mind-readers!" he said, running his hand through his slightly-thinning hair. "Lord knows I have enough trouble reading a book, let alone a mind!"

"So what'd you do this time?" said Irene, a statuesque blonde with a slow southern drawl.

"What do you mean what did I do this time? I did what men always do, the wrong fucking thing!" he said.

They'd all laughed and, a little later, when he came back to the table to report that an attempt at a cell phone apology had gone exceptionally badly, they laughed a little more.

Emma was slowly starting to feel at ease, enjoying sitting and listening to everything going on around her.

"You also the designated driver?" Her thoughts were interrupted by Alan from across the table.

"Sorry?"

"I see you're not drinking either. Fancy some non-alcoholic champagne?" he said, holding up a frosted green bottle.

"No it's not drinking and driving that's worrying me, it's drinking and drinking. I had a few too many with Stacey over dinner last night. I'm still recovering."

"A night out with Stacey? Ah, say no more," he smiled. He

reached out for her glass and poured what, in effect, was carbonated grape juice.

"Thanks," she said, taking the glass from him and raising it in a toast.

Half-way through the evening Emma had the strangest feeling come over her, a mixture of sad alienation she couldn't quite place. What was she doing here among virtual strangers so far from home? She suddenly needed fresh air and silently pushed her chair away from the table and walked outside onto the balcony.

Maybe it was the downer from the alcohol of the previous night, maybe it was being away from Daniel, her fearsome but familiar jailer. Oh Lord, had she forgotten how to function on her own?

She was leaning with her elbows on the railing, looking out into the dark night, when she felt movement at her shoulder and looked around to see Alan walking towards her.

"I saw you get up and leave; are you OK?" he asked.

"Oh, yes, I'm fine; thanks for asking," she said, turning to face him. "Just feeling a little far from home."

"Worried about the kids?"

"I don't have kids." He was astute enough to notice the light die in her eyes as she said it.

"I'm sure he'll survive without you just this once. Why don't you come in and let me buy you another round of that incredibly expensive grape juice? I believe it's a fine vintage."

She smiled. "That would be nice, thanks," she said and started back towards the hall, Alan close behind her. "Sorry about you and your wife," she said, glancing back at him. "I hope everything's OK."

"Oh, I'm sure she'll be back to her cheerful self by the time I get home," he said with a sigh, pushing open the door, and then standing back to allow her through. "Not the first time, won't be the last."

They went back in and re-joined the table but didn't speak again until it was time to say good bye.

It was 3am, the end of the party, and she and Alan were the only two sober people there. Stacey was extremely drunk, laughing too loudly and behaving badly. She and Tom were fighting and he was sitting in a corner drinking and scowling darkly.

"You've outdone yourself again, love," said Alan, taking Stacey's hand and leaning in to kiss her on the cheek. "As your accountant I am, of course, horrified!"

"Oh, Alan darling!" she said with an exaggerated pout, "You can't leave yet, I haven't even danced with you."

"Even the band's packed up, babe; I think it's time to go home and face the music."

"You know you're the best and I love you," she said coming in close and squeezing his cheek before planting a rather lingering kiss on his lips.

"Now, now, love," he said in mock protest, gently pushing her back, "wouldn't want boy wonder getting his cape in a knot. I'm too old and decrepit to get involved in a lover's tiff."

She laughed and, as he turned to go, tweaked his bottom. He shook a finger playfully at her before waving good bye to everyone at the table and walking away.

Then, almost as an afterthought, he turned around and walked back towards Emma.

"Are you ready to leave?" he said, resting his hand on the back of her chair and leaning down slightly towards her.

"Have been for a while," she said looking up at him, "haven't partied this hard since I was in college. I don't know how to do it anymore."

"Want a lift? I don't think Stacey's going to be in much of a state to drive anyone anywhere. And as you saw I didn't drink a drop all evening. I'm a safe bet."

"I don't want to put you out, I'm staying at the Regal."

"No problem, it's on the way," he said, straightening up and stepping aside to give her space.

"Great, you're a star; thank you," she said, standing up, "I'll just tell Stacey."

Stacey smiled suggestively when Emma told her she'd be catching a ride with Alan.

"You kids have a good time now," she said, winking and blowing a kiss good bye. "See you in the morning."

Sitting next to Alan in the car she suddenly felt awkward. She couldn't remember the last time she'd been alone with a man like this.

"Wouldn't like to be Stacey in the morning," said Alan, trying to break the silence.

"I wouldn't worry too much about her; she's had good training; she'll probably be in better shape than us," she said, looking straight ahead of her.

"So how do you know each other?" asked Alan. He looked over at her but she kept looking straight ahead.

"We met in college. She was crazy back then too. I always envied her just a little – so confident, so free, lived life the way she wanted to."

"Don't you?"

"I don't think many of us do; we're too afraid what others will think."

She glanced shyly over at him and saw his slow smile, illuminated by the lights on the dash.

The smooth car ride, the comfortable leather seat at her back, the soft music on the radio and the lights rushing by put Emma in a relaxed mood. She was starting to enjoy herself and was sorry when, all too quickly, they pulled up at the hotel.

"Thanks so much for the lift," she said. "It was nice meeting you." She put her hand out and he shook it, smiling.

"My pleasure. Nice meeting you too, Emma. You sure you don't want me to see you in to the lobby?"

"No, no, I'll be fine, thanks, bye" she said a little too hastily, and stepped out of the car and headed towards the hotel door without looking back.

Only once she reached her room did the feeling of emptiness sweep over her. Although it had been short, she'd enjoyed talking to Alan, enjoyed quiet conversation with a man. She was surprised and a little horrified at herself and even found herself thinking she should have invited him into the hotel lobby for coffee.

She changed, removed her make-up and brushed out her hair, then stood looking at herself in the mirror for the longest time. Sometimes she really had no idea who she was.

Although she was exhausted, once she was in bed Emma lay

wide awake, unable to sleep, reliving the party, reliving her conversation with Alan, seeing again his slow smile.

Eventually she fell into a restless sleep.

Daniel was waiting for her at the airport the next day. He reached for her bag and gave her a perfunctory kiss on the cheek before leading the way briskly towards the car.

On the way home they hardly spoke. They didn't much these days, but she'd been away for three days, the longest they had been apart in almost eight years, and she expected him to at least want to know how the trip had gone.

"Had a good time then?" was all he offered, and she, wanting to say so much and not knowing where to begin, could only manage, "Yeah, it was good, really good."

CHAPTER
TWELVE

LIFE, FOR BETTER or worse, returned to normal. The thrill she'd felt from her brief time away slowly dissolved and, within a couple of weeks, it was as if she'd never been away. All that was left was a kind of hollow, a feeling of loss for something she hadn't even realised she was missing.

The morning the phone rang, less than two weeks after she got back, Miami was the furthest thing from her mind. She was at a colleague's desk going over some advertising figures. Janine, who sat at the desk opposite her, took the call then called her over from the other side of the open plan office.

"Emma, it's for you," she said, holding the phone in the air, one hand covering the mouthpiece.

"Thanks, I'm coming. Can you put it through to my desk?" Emma walked over, her head still full of figures.

When she answered the call, it was a man's voice.

"Hello, is that Emma?"

"Um, yes, it is." She had the phone wedged between her raised shoulder and her ear as she rummaged through some papers on her desk. When she looked over at Janine and saw she was watching her, she instinctively turned her back.

A nervous cough. "I don't know if you remember me, this is Alan, Alan Graham, from Miami."

Remember him? How could she not? She put the papers down, gripped the phone with her unsteady hand.

"Alan, yes of course I remember you. How nice to hear from you." Her legs felt weak and she perched on the edge of her desk to steady herself.

"I hope you don't mind me calling. I got your number from Stacey. Is this a bad time?" he said, sensing her apprehension.

A bad time? Yes, in every way this was a very bad time. She had never felt so vulnerable, so lonely.

"No, not at all," she said, then, in a vain attempt at sounding casual, added, "So, what's new?"

"Well I hope you don't think it's inappropriate. I just wanted to call and say how nice it was meeting you. It was definitely a high point in an otherwise pretty low day," he said.

She smiled. "Oh, yes, how were things when you got home? Did arriving at 3am worsen or improve your chances of a reprieve?"

"I think the answer to that one's in the question," and he gave a short laugh. "But I survived, we all survive."

"Oh good, glad to hear it."

An awkward silence.

"Um, you know I hardly know you but it was really nice talking to you, it made me realise it's been a long, long time since I had a proper conversation with a woman." He paused and she heard him take a breath. "Would it be OK if I e-mailed you some time, you know, just to talk? Oh God, this is sounding pathetic. Could you please save me from myself and say something?"

Emma laughed. "I enjoyed our chat too. It'd be great to stay in touch," the slightest pause, "as friends." She cringed once she said it, but could hear the smile in his voice when he echoed, "Yes, as friends."

She heard a phone ringing on his side of the line and he asked her to hold.

"Yes, I'm just on the other line. I'll be there in a minute."

Then he was back. "Sorry about that, a client's waiting downstairs. I'm going to have to go, but give me your e-mail address."

Once she put down the phone she sat on the desk for the longest time, a smile on her face she couldn't seem to wipe off.

She couldn't shrug off the nagging guilt, especially when Daniel came home that evening and she found there was yet one more thing she wouldn't be sharing with him over dinner.

That night she made a special effort to try and make conversation.

"How are things at work?"

"Hmmm?"

"Work, how's it going?"

He looked momentarily surprised, then glanced quizzically at her. "Fine, yeah, fine."

"How's the Berger case going?"

Again, the startled look, a little impatient now.

"Yeah, good."

And realising that was all she was going to get out of him she gave up and fell silent again.

Alan didn't write immediately. In fact Emma checked her e-mail for a full week before, at last, a message appeared in her inbox from Alan Graham, subject title "Hi".

She was a little taken aback by how rapidly her heart was beating in her chest as she double-clicked the mouse and opened the message.

Even though it was just a few lines it was written with warmth and Emma smiled as she read:

Hi,

Before writing you a long, boring thesis, just wanted to make sure I had the right e-mail address. It's been a little hectic around here, really looking forward to talking to someone friendly for a change. So hope you're out there somewhere. Write back when you can.

Alan

Emma had a vague recollection of the dynamics of men and women to know not to reply straight away. So she impatiently waited out what she figured would be the respectable space of two days before writing back. She re-wrote the short e-mail five times, reading and re-reading it to try and give it the right tone.

Hey,

Great to hear from you, I hope your hectic schedule has relented a little. Just been looking at Stacey's pix from the party – that was quite a night wasn't it? Can't remember the last time I was out till 3am, I'm still recovering! I meant to ask you, have you always lived in Miami? It was my first time there – what an amazing city, but I wonder what it's like living there? Are you happy?

Look forward to hearing from you again,
Emma

Dear Emma, (came back the response almost immediately)

Are you happy? That's the big question, isn't it? And I'd need a lot more time than I have to be able to answer adequately. Maybe some other time I'll attempt it. The simple and politically correct answer is, yes, I love Miami. I was born in Sarasota, moved here after college on the promise of a job. The job fell through but I was determined to stay and eventually found something else. I met my wife here, ended up buying a house and never left. I can't really imagine living anywhere else. As for the rest, can anyone say they are truly happy? Never used to be a cynic, but am beginning to wonder if it's a myth.
Hope you're having a good day,
Alan

It was a clear opening, and even though she'd considered ignoring it, she didn't.

She waited a day before replying.

Dear Alan,

I had a friend who once said contentment was a way of selling out, settling for what you have instead of aiming for more. I lived my whole life trying to attain that state where life gives you pleasure, happiness. It seems like a life-time pursuit and, at times, a futile one. I think, perhaps, we have to be grateful that some aspects of our lives are as we would wish them to be. It's probably impossible to have it all. At least that's my two-pence worth of wisdom for the day.
Take care,
Emma

Wow, that was deep! Left me speechless for one of the few occasions in my life. Can't see my way through the heap of work on my desk at the moment, will write a proper message as soon as I have a bit of free time.

Alan

And so began the weekly, then daily and, eventually, twice daily messages between them, each one prising open the lid on their lives just a little at a time.

Emma found herself relying more and more on their communication and, as these things go, the more they confided in one another the more the attraction between them grew.

It started in small ways at first, little hints, sexual innuendos, cheeky flirts, mostly on Alan's part.

Hey,

What are you wearing today? Am picturing you in that little black number I met you in.

Initially she made feeble attempts to try and put him off, all the time inwardly hoping it wouldn't work.

She'd let him know that while she was flattered, she was a married woman (she never went so far as to call herself happily married) and had never seen herself as the cheating type.

What exactly is the cheating type? You mean human? Lol.

He'd laugh good naturedly at her prudishness and promise to be good. Until the next time.

I dreamt of you last night. I know you've told me not to talk to you like this but I can't help it. Now you're even intruding on my dreams, do you have no shame, woman? ;-)

Alan, you're really going to have to stop this, you're so bad. And I'm so, so weak.

The chinks in her armour grew wider until, by the time December came, she had opened up to him completely.

And once she let down the barriers she was astounded how quickly he totally occupied her life.

I sometimes think I must be a really terrible person, talking to you like this behind my husband's back. I know it's wrong but, God, I just can't help myself, you're my addiction.

It was inevitable that it would eventually go further, that at some point the fever ignited by the messaging wouldn't be enough anymore. Before long they were phoning each other every opportunity they could get, stealing calls when they were at the office or away from the house and, as they became emboldened by passion, in an upstairs room, the bathroom, the garden, when their spouses were otherwise occupied.

But it wasn't enough. Alan was becoming more and more insistent that they meet up. And as much as she wanted the same she was terrified of taking the next step, happy to live in this realm of fantasy which, she'd irrationally convinced herself, was still safe, still not quite cheating. As long as they didn't meet, didn't touch, made love only in their fantasies.

"Look, babe, you're driving me insane, I can't think, I can't work, I can't eat, all I do is think about you. I need to see you, there has to be some way."

"Alan we've been through this before," she said. She was sitting on the stairs behind her office block. "I never go away, the first and only time I did was to Stacey's party, there's no way I could pull it off without arousing Daniel's suspicions."

"Oh God, Emma, who cares anymore? Do we really care? All I care about is seeing you, being with you. Don't you have another college friend turning 40? Can't you make up one?"

"You don't just make up college friends, I didn't have that many to start with."

"Well maybe you could pretend Stacey was having some kind of emotional crisis and you had to go see her? God knows it wouldn't be a lie – she's always lurching from one emotional crisis to another!"

"I don't know, I just don't know, give me some time to think about it."

"Not too long, babe, I can't wait too long."

They never spoke of a future together, neither suggested leaving their partners for each other. So what was it all about? Why were they willing to risk so much for the promise of so little? Sex? Was that all it was? Surely not, Emma kept reassuring herself, even as she worked out the best way of spinning a tale to Daniel.

It was early January. She and Daniel had spent a dismal Christmas and New Year, her one and only overriding objective the entire holiday being to try and find ways to talk to Alan. In a particularly daring moment she left Daniel watching television and sneaked upstairs to the bathroom to message Alan. He called her right back and they talked in breathless whispers while his wife carved the turkey downstairs.

On Boxing Day she guiltily started planting the seeds of the lie: she'd heard from Stacey, she said, she was having a hard time with the divorce.

No response from Daniel.

The next day: "This was the first Christmas after the divorce, I guess that's why Stacey is taking it hard." Again, nothing.

Over the course of the next week her conversation was peppered with talk of Stacey's emotional despair: her ex-husband was threatening to sell the house, she was lonely and lost, she really needed a friend, she'd heard her ex was dating a good friend of hers.

She was amazed how easily and fluidly the lies, once released, flowed.

Daniel seemed at best uninterested, at worst impatient.

Eventually she realised she'd have to take a more direct approach.

"I really think she needs a friend right now, I'm thinking of making a trip to Miami." Emma was sitting on the edge of the bed, watching Daniel lift his collar and wrap his tie around his neck in front of the dresser mirror. "I'd just never forgive myself if she did something foolish."

"You want to fly to Miami?" The first sign of interest.

"I'm thinking about it. What do you think?"

"Seems a little extravagant for a friend you've seen once in the last five years," he said, pausing momentarily before bringing the two ends of the tie together in front of him and then squinting down to wrap one over the other.

"That's the whole point. I haven't been there for her, wasn't there for her all through the hard times, the divorce, I feel pretty guilty."

A shrug as he flicked the long end of the tie under before threading it through the knot.

"I hope you've got the money for this little jaunt."

"I have a little saved up."

"Fine."

And so it was done.

And now that it was done she was terrified.

Alan was ecstatic and immediately began planning the logistics of their weekend. More lies, to his wife this time, a business meeting in Orlando, he'd be away for two nights.

It wasn't unusual for him to go away on business so he was saved having to elaborate on the lie.

The day finally dawned.

Emma thought how different she felt getting on the plane on her own this time. At one point she was so wracked by guilt and fear she almost pulled out, but explaining why she was cancelling the trip would have meant more lies she was in no state to concoct. Besides, above the anguish and crisis of conscience was a far stronger and more compelling emotion she could no longer contain.

Landing in Orlando and heading for the carousel to collect her luggage, her legs felt like jelly. She walked through to the arrivals hall and there he was waiting, the smile she'd memorised so well.

He stepped forward and pulled her longingly towards him, kissing her hard on the mouth.

CHAPTER THIRTEEN

EMMA WOKE TO the sound of steel thudding on hard soil. She looked out of the window and saw Calvin in the opaque early morning light digging up the driveway.

It was another beautiful day, dawn smudging the sky pink and gold. She dressed and went out into the clear morning, the brisk air tingling her bare arms and legs.

She walked over to Calvin and he looked up in surprise.

"Sorry, didn't mean to startle you."

"Ya up early."

"I could say the same of you."

"Too hot later," he said, lifting the pick over his head and bringing it down hard.

"She means a lot to you, doesn't she?"

"Wat?" an impatient frown, squinting as he glanced at her through the cloud of dust.

"Elizabeth, she's really important to you."

A grunt.

"Coffee?" she raised her voice over the thudding.

Another grunt which she took for a yes.

Emma went in to get the coffee, needing a strong hot cup as much as he did. It had been another restless night, thoughts of Alan racing through her head like a high speed train.

She filled the kettle and switched it on and, slowly getting to know her way around the kitchen, found two coffee mugs and a teaspoon.

Waiting for the kettle to boil she looked absent-mindedly around the kitchen and then she saw it. She wondered why she hadn't noticed it before. It was right there in full view.

She reached up on tip-toes, lifted it off the pelmet and held it in her hands, turning it around and around, hardly believing what she was seeing.

Memories ran through her mind once more, like video footage played on fast forward, grainy and blurred.

Two children sitting side-by-side on a step, watching, fascinated, as the man held the paint brush, the tool so strangely delicate in his large hands. With soft strokes he brushed paint from a palette in front of him onto the canvas and, as if by magic, a picture emerged from what had at first seemed like random waves of colour. First the outline of a pear-shaped face, then eyes, laughing and blue. Honey-coloured hair flying as she tossed her head back. A garden behind her stretching back as if to eternity, a paradise of light and colour.

"Who's that in the picture, Harry?"

"You know who it is, Emma," said Peter.

And Harry just smiled.

Once it was finished he left it out on a window ledge to dry and Emma spent the whole afternoon running back and forth to check on its progress. As the afternoon wore on and the paint dried, Emma imagined the picture coming to life; every time she looked at it her mother looked more animated, the light deepened and spread in her eyes, the garden behind her seemed to bloom brighter.

Harry had never given the picture to Margot. He'd kept it in the little room at the back where he hung up his overalls at the end of each day and boiled water for tea on a two-plate stove. Once, when Emma had run to the back to tell him her father was calling, she saw the picture on the rough wooden shelf he had set up along one wall, supported by a brick at each end. There, next to a green enamel mug sat the painting, a tiny slice of heavenly light in the dreary room.

Emma held the picture to her chest, trying to fathom the puzzle which made up her mother's life, the pieces she just couldn't seem to put together, no matter how hard she tried.

Then she walked outside to Calvin, the picture still held tightly against her.

"Where did this come from?"

Calvin looked up sharply, struck by her voice.

"Wat's it to ya?"

"This is my mother."

"Says who? Scheme it could be anyone."

"Where did you find it?"

"With the rest of his shit. I tossed it out but the o' queen fished it out of the bin, said she smaaked it. No accounting for taste I s'pose." And he went back to his work.

Ragged with emotion Emma lunged forward and went in to slap him but his instincts were lightning-quick. He dropped the shovel and caught her wrist in the air, gripping it tight. They stood there for what seemed like an eternity, Emma breathing heavily and fighting hard to keep back the tears.

Then, just as suddenly, he dropped her hand, muttering "Bitch" as he turned to pick up the shovel.

Furiously wiping angry, hot tears from her cheeks with the back of her hand, Emma stormed back to the kitchen, still clutching the picture to her chest.

By the time Elizabeth woke up, Emma had pulled herself together and put the painting back on the pelmet. Needing to keep herself busy she'd made a big breakfast of French toast and bacon, just like the breakfasts her mother used to make, the French toast soft and golden brown, sprinkled with sugar and cinnamon, the bacon crispy and hot.

She remembered the August holidays when spring was just waking up after a three-month winter. When every branch sported new shoots preparing for a sky of riotous scarlet and lavender as the frangipani and jacaranda trees blossomed overhead. Perfect mornings when they'd wake up at 6 to make sure they didn't waste a moment of the day. Playing in the garden in the soft sunshine until about 8 when they'd run breathlessly in for breakfast, completely famished.

Days like that seemed to be a joyous, never-ending cycle of eating and playing and laughter, Peter her constant companion, a fellow conspirator of all their mad childhood games and schemes.

"Oh my dear, what's all this?" said Elizabeth, trying to smooth down the springy grey wisps of hair escaping her bun. "You didn't have to go through such trouble. What a lazy old woman I am, sleeping late and getting up to a cooked breakfast! Don't think I remember the last time…" she trailed off.

"I'm glad, you deserve a break and God knows I was awake anyway," said Emma, pulling out a chair and indicating for her to take a seat. "Thought I may as well do something useful."

She decided not to say anything about the picture – she had caused enough drama in this house already. This was her battle.

But when Calvin was called in for breakfast and eventually skulked in, glistening with sweat and moody as hell, Elizabeth sensed the tension between them.

"How's it going out there, dear?" she asked, piling streaky bacon onto his plate.

A grunt.

"Good? Lovely, dear, glad to hear it," she said, nonplussed.

"And you, Emma dear? What are your plans for today?"

"There are a few things I want to do in town…is there still a flower market outside the City Hall? I'd really like to get a photograph of that."

"I'm sure there is, but I hardly go into town anymore. Calvin, don't you need to get cement for the drive way? I have a wonderful idea, why don't you go in with Emma, it will save me having to take you in, and you can show her around. She may have forgotten where things are."

They both protested at once, mumbling incoherent excuses Elizabeth didn't – or chose not to – hear.

"Well that's settled then," she sat back, slapping both hands on the wooden table.

The two women cleaned the kitchen while Calvin took a shower and changed out of his work clothes.

He appeared silently in the kitchen, dressed in cargo pants and a freshly-pressed golf shirt

"I'll just grab my bag," she said, making her best effort to sound natural, and they were soon in the car, sitting side-by-side in total silence.

"Well, looks like we're stuck with each other," she said at last, no longer able to take the tension. "Maybe we need to make an effort to get along, for the morning anyway."

The characteristic grunt.

"What is that anyway?"

"Wat's wat?"

"The grunt. Is it a yes, is it a no, is it a maybe? You use it for everything, I can't figure it out."

A grudging smile out of one corner of his mouth. "That's why I smaak it."

"Smaak means like, right?"

"Mmm."

"The slang, it's a mystery to me. Your Dad," she paused for a moment, "he had an accent but he never used slang, he always spoke proper English."

"Proper English huh? Spoken by *proper* Englishmen?" His voice was a sneer. "I'm not English and neither was my o' bali, so I don't know why he tried so hard all his life to be White."

"Tried to be White, what do you mean? Just because he spoke properly?" she said, glancing over at him as she drove.

"Coz he spoke 'proper'," he almost spat out the words, "coz he smaaked White ouens, White chicks. Played White. Like he was ashamed of who he was."

"I think you've got him wrong, Calvin. Harry may have been a lot of things but he wasn't trying to be someone, something else. He wasn't like that."

"Oh, and ya'd know, huh? Ya knew my o' bali so well that ya'd know wat he was trying to be or not trying to be? Ya don't know a fucking thing!" he said, slamming his palm on the dash in front of him. "You only know wat ya wanna know, see what ya wanna see. Did ya even know my o' bali had a family? Did ya know he had an o' queen, he had lighties? No, coz he was too busy playing happy family with ya and yours, why talk about his goffel brats?"

"Goffel? I don't even know what that means!"

"Coloured, mixed breed, half-cast, makarad, take your pick. All means the same thing!"

"Listen Calvin, I really don't know why every conversation between us needs to be so damn hard!" They'd stopped at a red light and she turned around in her seat to face him. "I know you had a shit deal when you were a kid but did you ever imagine that mine was no picnic either? Do you happen to remember how my childhood ended?" And she gripped the steering wheel tight and drove on as the light turned green.

"Jah, wateva. I didn't go to no fancy school, I graduated in slang." He was looking out of his window. "This is my language, this is how I praat and I never gonna change, not for nobody."

"It would take a brave person to try suggesting you should, Calvin. All I was trying to say was that sometimes I don't understand what you're saying."

"So tune me."

"Tell you? Yes, next time I'll tell you. Now can we put it behind us?"

Their first stop was the builder's warehouse to order five bags of cement. An elderly White man, beer belly slopping over his leather belt, came over to serve them, completely ignoring Calvin and asking Emma how he could help her.

Emma saw Calvin bristle again and quickly stepped back, indicating that he was the one with the query.

"Looking for cement and sink screws." Suddenly Calvin's bravado vanished. His voice was thin and unsure and he was shifting uneasily from one foot to the other. She watched as he and the salesman slipped into what looked like pre-arranged roles, actors given a part to perform and, on cue, taking their positions, one ingratiating, the other patronising, ingrained in them as deeply as the creases on well-worn leather seats.

He bullied Calvin into choosing over-priced screws and two extra bags of cement and followed him all over the shop, making it look more like policing than good customer care.

They were hardly out the door before Emma, unable to contain herself any longer, blurted out, "What the hell was that?"

"Wat?"

"Why did you let him treat you like that?"

"Like wat?"

"Come on Calvin, don't mess with me, don't tell me you don't know what was happening in there!" She'd stopped outside the door, facing him, the car keys in her hand. "Why did you let him treat you like that? Shit I can't say boo to you without getting my head bitten off but that man treated you like dirt and you just took it. I don't get it!"

"You don't get it," he said, turning to face her. "That's the first true thing ya ever said. Ya don't get it, ya'll never get it. Is wat I been trying to tell ya all along."

"No way, Calvin, no way! You're not going to get away with it by launching into one of your 'what an idiot Emma is' speeches!" she said, refusing to keep walking until he gave her a proper answer. "We already know how that worn-out old tale goes. Just answer me: why the hell did you allow that man to treat you like you were shit?"

"Wat did ya want me to do? Jump over the counter and wring his useless neck like I wanted to?" he said, twisting his broad hands in a strangling motion. "Coloured ouen kills White ouen. How do you think that'd go down? Oh, wait, we already know how that would go down, right?"

A smirk.

"Calvin, this isn't Rhodesia, this is Independent Zimbabwe, what the hell is going on? Why does everyone around here have to act like cave men?"

"Ya been away so long ya forgotten the good o' times which, surprise, surprise are the good new times too. Some things never change," he said and started walking back towards the car. "White is still right and goffel menses are the bottom of the shit pile."

"Menses?" She started walking too.

"Ouens...I mean people, people!" he said, waving his hands around. "The difference for goffel ouens in Zimbabwe is...there ain't no difference! We been too dark for the White ouens, too White for the Black ouens, the outcasts. Nobody wanted us then, nobody wants us now." They reached the car and he leaned up against the passenger door, waiting for her to unlock her side. "Car gets hucked? Musta been the goffel ouens, we know wat goffel ouens are like, always hucking stuff. That's just the way it goes down. See the way the o' bali followed me around the shop? Was making sure I wasn't hucking nothin'."

"Calvin, it's got to be more than that, this is just ridiculous, this is over 30 years after Independence, for God's sake." Emma had one hand on top of the car, the other on the door handle as she talked to him over the roof. "You can't judge a whole society on one loser guy in a hardware store. He talked you down and you let him. And I want to know why."

He curled his long body into the passenger seat, sat down and looked straight ahead. "Ya just don't get it," he said again. Then he turned and looked right at her. "Wat ya doin' tonight?"

"Tonight? Nothing, I'm not doing anything. Why?"

"I scheme it's time ya learnt some home truths, seen how the other half lives, if you think ya can handle the scandal."

"Handle the scandal?" she couldn't help but smile. "What do you have in mind?"

"Trust me."

CHAPTER
FOURTEEN

FROM THE HARDWARE store they drove to the City Hall where a flower and curios market on the sidewalk outside was still one of the city's most popular tourist attractions.

Emma remembered the day she went there with her father to buy flowers. It was January. Hot and humid. The sky a brooding blue canopy overhead. The kind of day that would boil and brew all morning until lunch time, when soft white clouds would begin to drift lazily across the sky, gathering so stealthily you wouldn't even realise they were there…until the light shifted and the first, fat raindrops fell to the ground with loud splats.

The flower market was a welcome shelter from the stinging heat of the car, and the children loved being under the shade of the canopy of jacaranda trees, surrounded by the sweet scent of freshly-cut roses and carnations, set in green and blue plastic buckets of water, lifted up, dripping-wet, by eager salesmen and thrust in their faces.

It was alive with voices and scents and colours, a whirling mass of buyers and sellers, each trying to outdo the other.

"Hello boss, fresh red roses for the nkasana – the little girl – look, nice and fresh, look, look," said an old Black woman, whistling through the gaps in her toothless smile, her face sunken in like a sponge cake taken out of the oven too soon. She wore a length of brightly-coloured cloth tied under her armpits and as she waved the roses the loose skin under her upper arms rippled and shook.

"Carnations, Mama, look, beautiful carnations, I give you good price, come see, good, good price," a slim, young man knelt down to look into Emma's face, long, fat dreadlocks spinning around his head as he gestured to the yellow carnations on his stand.

Peter and Emma wanted to stop at every stand to admire the flowers and smell the bunches held out to them. But their father was irritable and impatient, batting away the bunches of flowers like he was swatting at flies, snarling at the over-enthusiastic sellers trying to persuade him to stop at their stand.

Finally, after walking the entire length of the market and checking on both sides of the crowded sidewalk, he found what he was looking for: pure, white rose buds. An elderly man, with a streak of white right down the centre of his otherwise jet-black hair, sat quietly on a three-legged wooden stool calmly tending to his roses. Gently extracting each snow white stem from the bucket in front of him, he expertly snipped off the lower leaves and arranged them in a bunch which he wrapped in gold cellophane.

He barely looked up when they approached.

Her father stood in front of him, his fists clenched at his sides, Emma and Peter on either side.

"How much?"

The old man, in no hurry to leave his work, slowly lifted his head and looked at their father.

"Heh?" he said, wrinkling up his nose.

"I said," he raised his voice, making no effort to hide his irritation, "how much for the flowers?"

A slow, lazy smile.

"Twenty dollars a stem." At least double the price of all the other flower sellers.

"What? Are you insane? That's daylight robbery!"

The old man merely shrugged his shoulders and went back to his work.

"Enough wasting my time, what's the real price?"

"Twenty dollars," he said again, without even looking up.

"You people are all the same, God-damn thieves, all of you!"

No response.

"Come on children," he said, hoping the sign of his departure would encourage the old man to call him back and reduce the price. But the flower seller didn't budge.

They took two or three steps and then her father swung angrily around, stormed back and tossed a wad of $20 bills at the old man's feet.

"Give me 12!"

The old flower seller smiled slowly and, taking his time, handed him a bunch of roses. Her father grabbed them from him and, muttering under his breath about "filthy kaffirs", turned to leave. Emma, having watched the transaction with wide eyes, was close behind him.

Suddenly a bony hand grabbed her wrist and she swung around to find herself face-to-face with the old man.

No lazy smile now, a hard, cruel glint of hatred in his eyes that scared Emma so badly she couldn't even cry out.

The old man brought his mouth close to her ear and whispered, his breath foul, "I'm going to kill you and your racist pig father. And if you tell anyone, I'll kill you very, very slowly."

With that he let go of her wrist so fiercely she almost lost her footing and, close to tears of fear and panic, stumbled after her father and Peter. By the time she reached them they were nearly at the car and hadn't even noticed her absence. Peter realised she was upset, but when he asked her why she just bit her lip and said she wanted to go home, she was hot and she wanted to see Mama.

She never told a soul about the old man's threat, but stayed awake for several nights afterwards waiting to hear the approaching footsteps of their killer.

When he didn't come, she eventually relaxed and might have forgotten about the incident altogether had it not been for the nightmares. They started soon afterwards and were always the same. It was late afternoon, the sun a violent red slash across the sky. She and Peter were sitting in the mulberry tree picking berries. They could hear their mother calling but ignored her. As the sun died and the shadows lengthened, her calls began to die down and, eventually, stopped altogether.

Suddenly they heard a rustling of leaves and a dark form appeared, scrambling up the tree towards them. It was the old man from the flower market, the glint of hatred burning in his eyes. His lips were pulled back, exposing yellowing teeth as large and perfectly square as ripe corn kernels. She could smell his foul breath. As he stretched long, talon-like fingers towards her, Emma saw that his hands were covered in what at first looked like mulberry stains but, as he drew closer and lurched towards her, she realised was blood. She screamed and lunged away from him, tumbling out of the tree, leaving Peter up in the branches to fend off the killer alone.

She always woke up before hitting the ground.

After the accident, although the sequence of events never changed, sometimes in her dreams the old flower seller would be replaced by Harry, an ugly Harry with murder in his eyes.

In adulthood, thinking back to the old man at the flower market, she wondered if it had happened at all or was just a figment of her overactive childhood imagination, fuel for the nightmares which haunted her nights.

As for the roses, bought for her mother as a peace offering after a particularly bitter argument which the children had heard raging late into the evening, Emma was playing by the mulberry tree the next day and, seeing something sticking out of the garbage bin at the back, went over and peeped inside. There were the roses, their delicate white buds crushed and stamped before they'd had a chance to bloom.

CHAPTER
FIFTEEN

ELIZABETH WAS SITTING on the porch when they arrived back at the house and she smiled to herself when she saw them get out of the car, talking. She smiled again when Emma casually announced they'd be going out together that evening.

"Oh lovely, dear, I'm so glad."

They ate an early dinner with Elizabeth and, afterwards, Emma excused herself to shower and change.

Not sure what Calvin had in store for her or where they would end up, she chose a pair of bootleg jeans and a fitting red t-shirt. She stepped back from the full length mirror in her room and appraised herself, smoothing down her t-shirt, tugging her jeans down where the fabric was bunching up on her inner thighs, turning sideways to despair at the bulges.

Then she smiled sadly to herself, remembering how much Alan had liked her curves, how he'd made her feel, for the first time in her life, beautiful and desirable. How he'd smothered all her protestations about her weight with kisses, how, wherever she was in the room, his eyes would be on her, watching her every move, drinking her in, devouring her.

The first time she'd felt something wasn't quite right was when she was cutting the beef fillet she'd cooked for Sunday lunch, about three cold, lonely weeks after her return from Orlando.

She'd been trying to deal with all the conflicting emotions, the longing like a cold, heavy stone in her chest, the loneliness, the guilt. And then, while carving the roast, an odd feeling. The smell of it was overpowering and she felt like retching. The feeling passed and she didn't think any more about it.

Until the queasiness began. She'd feel dizzy, light-headed, if she stood up too quickly. It felt like her food was sitting in her throat, never quite going down.

She finally decided to go in for a check-up. The diagnosis was the last thing she expected.

Emma sat across from the doctor, one of several in the family practice she'd been visiting for years, and thought she heard him wrong when, after giving him a run-down of her symptoms, he asked when she had had her last period.

"Sorry? "Her brows furrowed.

"Well it might just be a good idea to rule out all possibilities, when was your last menstrual cycle?"

"Um, I'm sorry, I really couldn't tell you, I'm not so good at keeping a track of it."

"Well then, what I'd like to suggest is a pregnancy test" and, before she could protest, he was standing up and walking to the door to call the nurse. After giving her a few instructions he turned to Emma. "If you'll go with Nurse Parker she'll show you what to do and I'll see you back here afterwards."

Emma was too stunned to speak. Like a robot, she followed the nurse to the procedure room where, with shaking hands, she took the plastic jug and walked, as instructed, to the tiny, slightly stale-smelling toilet where she was to take a urine sample.

The rest of the day passed in a blur. She had a vague recollection of handing her urine sample to the nurse and waiting in the reception area where she tried her best not to make eye contact with any of the other patients. Her heart was beating uncontrollably in her chest and, when her name was finally called out, her legs were almost too weak to carry her back to the doctor's door.

He looked up at her as she walked in and smiled kindly and, although she tried desperately, she couldn't gauge anything from his expression. After what seemed like an eternity, he coughed slightly and declared: "Well Mrs Groves, your pregnancy test has come back positive."

She felt as if the ground beneath her had given way, and she started to tremble.

"Are you sure?" she asked.

"Well these tests are 90 percent accurate. However, the most reliable method of testing is taking blood, not urine."

"Then I want to have a blood test."

"Are you sure about that? The results from the urine sample, coupled with the symptoms you're experiencing, all tie up, it's probably not necessary. What I can do is send you for a scan to see how far along you are."

But she insisted on the blood test anyway and sat again, stunned and speechless, when that too came back positive.

Next was the scan, and she was struck by the irony. What she wouldn't have given during the early years of her marriage to Daniel to go for a scan and have the technician point out the tiny cell swimming in her womb and tell her that that was her child. The pain of accepting that she would probably never have children had eventually died and, along with it, any intimacy she and Daniel had shared. And just when she had given up the idea of having a child of her own, it was happening...but not with Daniel.

Terrified by the implications, she stumbled out of the doctor's offices and the minute she sat in her car, called Alan.

Hearing his voice on the other end was a momentary balm and she burst into tears.

"Emma! What's the matter? Why are you crying?"

"Oh God, Alan! Oh God, oh God! I can't!" She was crying so hard she couldn't get the words out.

"Just calm down, honey, tell me what's wrong, what's going on? Are you hurt? Has Daniel found out?"

"No," she said, "but he will!"

"What do you mean?"

"Oh Alan, I'm pregnant!"

She heard a sharp intake of breath on the other end of the line and then silence.

"Alan, Alan, are you there?"

"Yes, yes I'm here, I'm just speechless. I don't know what to say. Um, Emma, I thought you said you couldn't have children?"

"That's what the doctors always said, we couldn't have children, and because I'd had menstrual problems my whole life we both figured it was me."

"Did you go for tests?"

"Yes, urine, blood, I had a scan, I saw the baby!" A fresh round of sobs.

"No, I mean at the time when they said you couldn't have children, did you do tests?"

"We started and then things were just so bad between Daniel and me they petered out. Oh, Alan, what are we going to do?" She had her head down, her forehead resting on the top of the steering wheel.

"God I don't know, it's all a bit much to take in, I need to think. Let's just take a couple of days to think. Are you OK?"

"No, Alan, I'm not OK! I'm scared and I'm sick and my breasts hurt!" She was crying again.

"Calm down hun, you're going to have to calm down or Daniel will suspect. You're going to have to pull yourself together and let's think this through carefully."

By the time she disconnected the call she was feeling a little calmer.

She mustered all the self-control she had, went home and faced Daniel.

She'd never been so grateful for the distance between them. As was the case most nights, Daniel seemed barely to notice she was there. He came through the door by seven, wolfed down his dinner and retreated to his office where she imagined she could hear the computer quietly hum all the way through the night. He often slept on the couch there and, in the morning, after a rushed breakfast, would head out the door again.

Alan didn't call for the next two days. She lay awake at night, wracked with fear and panic and unable to sleep, waking up in the morning, tired, worn-out and nauseous.

She sent him several text messages and received short but warm replies that he was tied up in meetings and would call as soon as he got a moment alone.

He finally phoned about lunch time on the third day, and Emma was so relieved she almost started to cry again.

He heard the tremor in her voice and urged her to try and stay calm.

"Emma, I've thought about nothing but the pregnancy since you called, it's doing my head in thinking about it. Hun, I really don't see a solution that wouldn't involve destroying everyone around us, my wife, my kids, your marriage. I don't think we can do this, realistically I don't think I can do it."

"What are you saying, Alan?"

"I think maybe we should consider an abortion." He spilt out the words in a rush.

"What?" She couldn't believe what she was hearing.

"An abortion, babe, surely you've thought about it?"

"An abortion? No, Alan, honestly-speaking, it didn't even cross my mind!"

"So what did you think we were going to do, Emma? Run off into the sunset and raise a child together? Come on, love, we have to be realistic. We're not youngsters anymore, we can't do this. You're 42 years old, for God's sake! There are so many health risks, to you and the baby."

Silence on the other end. Frankly she didn't know what to say. She felt scared and angry, angry with Alan for picking the easy way out, angry with herself for being so naïve.

"Hun, are you there?"

"Yes I'm here," she said, her voice thin.

"Baby, I know you're hurting, I am too. But I think we have to be practical. Can't you see that? Can't you see how impossible it would be to go through with it?"

"I need to think Alan, I can't do this right now. I just can't do this."

"OK babe, you take some time to think, but remember there's a time limit to these things."

"These things?" She almost spat out the words.

"Abortions, babe, there's a time limit, you want to do it as soon as possible. Look, hun, right now it's not really a baby at all, it's just blood. Now's the time to do it, before it develops. You know it makes sense."

"No, Alan, it doesn't make sense, none of it makes any sense. Look, I'll call you." And with that she cut the call.

She couldn't get the words out of her head: it's just blood.

Yet, realistically, how was she going to raise a child alone? Daniel would divorce her and leave her with nothing, Alan was making it obvious adultery was as far as he'd go in jeopardising his marriage.

What kind of life would she be able to offer this child? How could she possibly give it a fair chance?

A week after the initial doctor's appointment Emma looked up the address of a family planning clinic in another county, not wanting to run the risk of bumping into anyone she knew.

She'd hardly had any contact at all with Alan over the last week. He had tried to call once or twice but she'd pretended she was busy and kept the conversations short and unemotional.

"Have you made a decision, babe? I want you to know I'm here for you."

She didn't reply. Where was he as she lay night after endless night, clutching her stomach and dreaming of the life inside her? He certainly wasn't there when she walked into the softly-lit waiting room of the family planning clinic and approached the window at reception.

"Um, I need to speak to a counsellor," Emma told the woman behind the desk.

She was led to a private room, painted clinical white, a pastel print on the wall and soothing piped music coming through speakers in the corner. There was a round table with three chairs and an examination bed.

Emma took a seat and waited. After about 10 minutes a nurse came in and introduced herself as Catherine. She was about Emma's age, short and plump, with a round matronly face and kind eyes behind thick glasses.

"How can we help you, dear?"

And then it all came spilling out.

"I'm six weeks pregnant. My husband is not the father. I don't think the father is going to take responsibility, he's married. It's not what he planned."

"Is it what you planned?"

"God no! I thought I couldn't have children. All those years my husband and I tried. Nothing. Now I'm over 40, I don't think I can do this alone."

"You've come in to discuss an abortion."

She looked down, nodded almost imperceptibly.

"Are you sure?" she asked.

"I'm sure I can't have a baby alone. I know that makes me weak but I'm so alone and I know nothing about children, I'm old for God's sake!" She looked at the woman, not sure if she wanted her to agree or protest. "What would you do if you were me, Catherine?"

"I can't answer that, my dear. Your reasons are your own, I'm not here to judge or question them. If you have reservations, strong reservations, and you've thought them through, then they're valid. I'm here to help you facilitate whatever route you plan to take."

"What are my options?"

"There's a surgical and a medical procedure."

She was only half listening as Catherine went into a detailed description of the two options.

Part of her wanted to do it right there and then, get it over and done with, but the other part wasn't ready, probably never would be.

So she came back to the clinic three days in a row, each time planning to pay her money and have the abortion, each time ending up sitting with Catherine for sometimes up to an hour, and leaving without resolving anything.

But on the fourth day, a conversation with Alan helped make up her mind.

"Alan, it's killing me, this decision. I really need you. I need to see you, talk to you. Is there any way?" She was sitting at her dressing table, staring at her tear-streaked face in the mirror.

"Oh baby, there's nothing in the world I'd like more. But right now? I can't get away, it's just not possible."

"I can't do this alone Alan. Please." She rested one elbow on the dresser and covered her tired eyes, rubbing them hard.

"If you can hang on a week or two, babe, maybe I can make a plan, but not now, no way."

"If we're going to go ahead with this abortion we have to do it soon. You said so yourself. Remember, while it's still nothing but blood? Your words!" She sat up straight and opened her eyes.

"All I'm saying is now isn't a good time for me."

"Yeah, Alan, and it's a freaking fantastic time for me. OK, thanks, I get the message!" She stood up, started walking towards the door, the phone still in her hand. "I know I tend to be a little slow on the uptake but I'm finally hearing you, loud and clear, I'm in this alone!" Feeling giddy she felt for the dresser stool and sat again. "I am such an idiot! Good bye Alan." And she cut him off for the second time in a week, then sat with her head in her hands for a long time.

Emma drove to the clinic that day. Later she had no recollection how she got there but, when she did, she'd dried her tears and steadied her shaking hands.

She asked to see Catherine and, when she came around the corner, took a deep breath and without any preliminaries announced: "I'm ready."

The piped music coming through the loud speaker into the small sterile room was Ave Maria. Catherine's hands were warm, her voice gentle. Emma closed her eyes tight and squeezed tears through the cracks.

She had a vision of her mother's white roses: buds crushed before they had a chance to bloom.

CHAPTER
SIXTEEN

EMMA'S MOOD WAS distinctly morose when she came out of the room to look for Calvin. She was beginning to think this was a bad idea and was wishing she hadn't agreed. But it was too late now. Besides, she didn't really want to be alone with her thoughts, maybe a distraction would do her good.

Calvin was waiting in the lounge, talking to Elizabeth. They both turned around when she came in and Calvin instinctively started to stand up before catching himself and sitting back down again.

"No, no, don't stand up," she said with a smile as he grunted.

Elizabeth saw them off and, giving Emma a key to get in, locked the door behind them.

She smiled, feeling like a teenager again.

Initially, the only words between them were Calvin's directions. Emma had no idea where they were going and was concentrating on the dark roads.

"Let's jol in here," said Calvin as he directed her to the only free parking outside a lively bar on the main street that ran through the city.

The flag of a local soccer team fluttered at the door and a man looking more like a hobo than a security guard offered to watch the car.

At the doorway a bouncer loomed over them and raised one eyebrow just a fraction when he saw Calvin come in with Emma.

"Crab," he said, tapping his fist on his heart by way of greeting.

"Bones, wat's the story my china?" said Calvin, jerking his chin.

They wove their way through the thick cloud of smoke and noise until they reached the bar. There was only one free bar stool so Calvin indicated for her to take it while he stood beside her.

"Crab?"

"Nickname," he said, giving no other explanation.

"And Bones?"

"Ya don't wanna know." He smiled slightly.

A giant of a man behind the bar greeted Calvin and they exchanged an intricate hand shake and a conversation so riddled with slang there was hardly a recognisable word in it.

"Wat's ya poison?" he asked her over the noise.

"Huh?"

"Ya poison? Wat is it? Wat ya drinking?"

"Do they have Amarula?"

"Amarula! That's fuckin' baby's milk!"

"I'm starting slow."

He shrugged, ordered an Amarula for her and a beer for himself.

A massive flat screen TV in one corner of the bar was showing a live soccer match and a crowd had gathered around to watch.

Calvin, beer in hand, wandered over to get a better look, leaving her on her own by the bar. She was sandwiched between a beefy man wearing a vest and a woman in skinny jeans, a halter neck top and hair extensions to her waist which she kept tossing in Emma's direction as she flirted with the man beside her.

Even on her own Emma felt strangely comfortable, slowly sipping the sweet cold liqueur, watching the people around her, catching snippets of conversations.

The woman next to her giggled as her date leaned closer and whispered in her ear, his hand moving higher up her thigh. She threw back her head, tossing her hair again, and placed her hand over his, Emma couldn't quite tell whether to encourage or stop him.

She felt something brush against her shoulder and swung around to see the beefy man had slid his bar stool a little closer to her and was beaming inches away from her face.

"Hello," he said with a wink, one gold tooth gleaming. "What's your name?"

He was a little too close for comfort, his shoulder practically touching hers, but she was more amused than threatened.

Seeing him this close-up, she noticed the pock marks on his otherwise smooth ebony face, like tiny potholes on new tar. His skin was so dark and shiny it was reflecting the overhead lights, and his teeth blazed white as he smiled.

"Emma," she said, feeling relaxed enough to go with a friendly approach.

"Emma. A beautiful name, for a beautiful woman."

He rested his forearm on the counter between them, flexing his muscles slightly and raising one eyebrow.

"I'm Joseph." His voice was dark caramel.

"Hello Joseph."

"You're American." A statement, not a question.

"Now I am, yes."

"And before?"

"Zimbabwean. I was born here."

He leaned backwards to take a better look at her, his eyes wide.

"No! Don't tell me!"

"Why's that so hard to believe?"

"You know why."

"No I don't, tell me."

"Look around you lady," he said with a sweeping gesture of his hand, "do you see any White Zimbabweans around here, socialising with us? It doesn't happen."

"But surely things are different now."

"Jah," he gave a deep chuckle, "now you can get arrested if you call a Black man the 'k' word. But nothing's changed in here," he said touching his heart with his clenched fist and growing suddenly solemn. "But enough serious stuff, let's talk about you, Emma. Are you here alone?"

"No, I'm here with a friend, he's over there watching soccer."

"And he left a beautiful lady like you alone? He's not scared you'll be stolen away?"

"I guess he thinks I can look after myself," said Emma, running her finger up and down the liqueur glass, making streaks through the frost.

Calvin had glanced over and seen her talking, then turned back to the screen. But when he looked again a few minutes later and they were still talking, Joseph inching closer and closer, he sighed, reluctantly left the game and walked over.

"Can't leave ya alone for two minutes," he said into her left ear as he sidled up to her.

"What? I'm fine."

"Hey bra, wat's the story?" he jerked his chin in Joseph's direction.

"No story makarad, just talking to this lovely lady here."

"Wat d'ya call me, china?"

"I called you makarad. You got a problem with that, makarad?" Joseph smiled broadly.

"No china, I got no problem. You the one with the problem when I get done with you." Calvin's voice was low and deadly.

"Calvin, it's cool, everything's cool," said Emma.

Then Joseph made his fatal error. He reached over and grabbed Calvin's arm.

Calvin violently flung his arm up, shaking off Joseph's hand.

"Wat the fuck ya doing? Don't ya touch me, don't ya fucking touch me! I'm gonna fuck ya up, d'ya hear me?"

Calvin's eyes were wild and all other noise in the pub seemed to die away.

Within minutes the bouncer was at his side, restraining him and pushing him towards the exit, Calvin resisting at first but eventually allowing himself to be led out.

Emma was right behind him and when he made a move to go back in and finish what he'd started, she barred his way and refused to let him.

"Let it go, Calvin! Shit, all of a sudden you go all Neanderthal on me! I was handling the situation, I didn't need rescuing."

"Huh? Rescuing? Don't flatter yourself, I wasn't rescuing no-one. Ya didn't know wat ya was getting yourself into, I just didn't wanna be picking up the pieces afterwards."

"Oh, so you were worried about me?" And she smiled.

A grunt. "Come on, let's get the fuck outta here."

"Where to next, Crab?" she said as she unlocked the car door and stepped inside, and he gave her a sideways look.

They moved on to another pub in a much quieter part of town, with long benches set out on a wooden deck overlooking a miniature lake.

Calvin held on to her elbow and steered her through the busy entrance to a bench.

"This is better," she said, sitting down and looking up at the sky. "You don't see stars like this anywhere else in the world."

"Might not have enough action for ya, no druggies for ya to chat up," said Calvin as he sat down opposite her.

"Druggies?"

"Yes Mrs 'I-can-handle-my-own-shit'. Wat ya don't know 'bout your new squeeze is that he's one of the biggest dealers in town. Ya really know how to pick 'em don't ya?"

"I didn't pick him, he picked me!" she said, feeling light-headed on the one glass of Amarula and laughing as she spoke.

"Right," he said. "So you ready to move on from baby's milk?"

"Yeah, I think I am. A vodka and orange please. I can see I'm going to need some fire to keep up with you tonight."

Calvin stood up to find a waiter, glancing back briefly before he left.

When he came back they sat in comfortable silence, sipping their drinks. They seemed, for the time being at least, to have slipped into a quiet ease with one another.

At first she didn't recognise the ring tone as her own, but as it grew louder she realised it was coming from her bag and reached down to pull it out.

"Hello? Hi!" hearing Alan's voice on the other end of the line she stood up and walked to the railing of the deck as she talked. Calvin watched her go. "Hey, this is a surprise, how are you?"

They only spoke for about five minutes as the line was distant and crackling and, at the end, Emma felt somehow sad and disconnected.

Straight after the abortion she'd stopped taking his calls altogether. She was in a deep depression and Alan was the last person she wanted to talk to. Although she'd made the final decision, she resented him for forcing her hand and leaving her to face it alone.

There was guilt too, and intense loss for what might have been. All she could feel was an overwhelming and unreasonable need to go home…to Zimbabwe.

Alan persisted through all her attempts to shrug him off and, eventually, she found herself turning back to him. But she was guarded. He tried to persuade her to risk taking another trip to meet him but she wasn't ready, kept putting him off. It still stung that when she really needed him he hadn't been there.

He couldn't believe it when she told him she was going to

Africa, but since she hadn't told him anything about her life before she arrived in the States, there seemed no point even trying to explain to him why she was doing it.

She came back to the table and Calvin raised his eyebrows almost imperceptibly as she sat down.

"Did I miss anything?"

"Nah, your boyfriend hasn't come looking for ya yet. But he'd probably have to take a number and queue," he said, throwing back his head to drain the last sip of his beer from the can.

"What's that supposed to mean?"

"Nothin'."

"Don't give me that, everything you say means something," she said, not quite sure why she was confronting him.

"I don't care wat shit ya up to, it's none of my business."

"You got that right."

They sat in heavy silence for a few minutes.

"So does your o' man know?"

"What?"

"Does your o' man know ya messin' around?"

"What happened to it being none of your business?"

"I'll take that as a no." He put his empty beer can to one side and started looking around absent-mindedly at the other tables.

"You know you've got a real nerve!"

He glanced back at her, startled by her tone, and smiled.

"Scheme I touched a nerve." Still smiling, he stood up to get another drink. "You ready for another one?"

"No!" she said, still bristling.

"Suit yourself." And he walked off.

Emma sat there simmering, realising full well that guilt, more than anything else, was driving her anger. She began to regret her outburst but there was no chance of making amends since he wasn't alone when he came back.

He had a tall, lanky youth with him, jeans worn low on his hips, trainers with no socks, a baseball cap worn back to front.

"Meet Elroy, my cuz," he said when they returned. "Elroy's also into the goods, thought maybe ya'd like to meet him."

"I don't do drugs, Calvin, but nice to meet you anyway, Elroy," she said.

Elroy reached around the back of his head to raise his baseball cap in an incongruous show of courtesy, but didn't bother taking out the cigarette dangling from the corner of his mouth. From behind a cloud of smoke, eyes half-closed, he mumbled, "Wassup?"

He took a seat next to Emma so they both sat facing Calvin, and the two men carried on a conversation which, once again, had Emma completely dumbfounded.

She sat quietly sipping her drink, until, suddenly, through snippets of their conversation, she realised the subject had changed to her, they were talking about her right there at the same table.

She heard the words "fine honey" and Elroy was staring at her. Calvin just gave a bored shrug.

"Are you talking about me?" she asked.

"Jah, 'bout ya, not to ya," Calvin said and they both laughed. Emma rolled her eyes.

"My boy Elroy's gotta be joling cabin now," said Calvin, ignoring Elroy's protestations, "it's way past his bed-time, ain't it El?"

"Aw, come on Crab," said Elroy and his voice was peevish.

"Ya heard me Elroy, head!"

And with a petulant sigh, shoulders drooping, Elroy stood up and left.

They watched him sulk off.

"How old is he? He only looks about 18," said Emma as they watched him slouch off.

"Ya giving him way too much credit, Elroy's just turned 15."

"Fifteen, and dealing drugs? You were joking about that right?"

"Nah, ain't nothin' to joke 'bout. Elroy's dealin' drugs alright. Been dealin' 'em since he was 13. Introduced to them by Uncle Conkey."

"Uncle Conkey?"

"My o' queen's big bro, liked to keep it in the family did good o' Uncle Conkey."

"Liked? He's dead?"

"Probably be a good thing if he was. Nah, Uncle Conkey got remarried, got himself a young honey and a lightie. Training him up to be just like his o' man I scheme. Welcome to the family," and he raised his beer can in a toast.

"How about you? Didn't he ever try to get you into the family trade?"

"Wat ya scheme? Scheme I'd be the kind, huh? Pushin' drugs seem like my thing?"

"No, I didn't say that. I just asked."

"Seems like that'd be too much like hard graft. Rather take them than push them," and he winked, so she wasn't sure whether or not he was joking.

"Elizabeth says you have two sisters."

"Jah, wat 'bout 'em?"

"No, nothing, I was just wondering, how old are they, what do they do?"

"Ya aks a lot of fucking questions. My sisters ain't up for discussion, subject closed. Now ya smaak another drink or wat?" He ordered another round of drinks and they sat in relative silence again. Talking to him was like treading a field littered with land mines, you never knew when you'd step on one and it would blow up.

Another half hour and Emma was starting to feel a little cold. A breeze had picked up, cooling as it blew over the lake and making the hairs on her arms stand up.

"Ya cold?" said Calvin noticing her shiver slightly.

"A little."

"Ready to jol?"

"Sure."

"I scheme we've given it enough time, the Club should be pumpin' by now."

"The Club?"

"Ya'll see."

CHAPTER
SEVENTEEN

"THE CLUB" WAS the popular name for the community hall in the suburb of Somerset, designated in pre-Independence Zimbabwe as the Coloured area.

A solid, square, unadorned building, it was the venue of weddings, 21st birthday parties, New Year's Eve dances, dart championships and Friday night Battle of the Bands competitions. The residents never complained about the noise – most of them were out at the Club anyway – and more than one baby had been conceived in its dark, dusty parking lot.

As they approached – the local mosque at one end of the narrow street, a Catholic Church at the other – Emma could feel the bass thumping.

The crowd had spilt out of the doorway and into the parking lot. A few stragglers were scattered on the road leading in, another handful were leaning up against their cars or walking hand-in-hand into the tangled scrub that formed its back boundary.

A woman with a baby in a pram, curlers in her hair, stood shouting at a man with a beer in one hand, a cigarette in the other. He stared at the ground while she bellowed.

A group of teenage girls stood in a huddle at the doorway, trying to look older than they were, flaunting their stringy young bodies in skirts so short they had to keep pulling them down.

Two teenage boys stood to one side ogling them, full of budding sexuality they had no idea what to do with.

A particularly attractive girl at the centre of the group caught Calvin's eye and called out to him, waving wildly.

She broke away from the group and came tripping over in impossibly high heels.

"Calvin, Calvin baby, you didn't call!" It didn't look right, adult sensuality on her wide-eyed little girl face.

"Jah, I didn't."

"But you promised."

"Sherise, I never make promises, then I never gotta keep 'em. Ya must know that 'bout me by now."

She was gently gripping his arm, pressing her body against his, batting her eyelashes and pouting.

"But baby…"

Then out of the corner of her eye she saw Emma, standing just to the side of Calvin.

"Who the fuck is this?" Her voice was shrill.

"Sherise, meet Emma," and Calvin smiled.

"Nice to meet you," but Emma's proffered hand was ignored as Sherise looked her up and down.

With a final fierce look Sherise focused her attention back on Calvin.

"Didn't you have a good time?" Her voice was soft again and

she was running a finger along his chiselled jaw line.

"I always have a good time, ya know that." Then gently but firmly he extracted himself from her grasp and, grabbing Emma's hand, started moving towards the door again.

"Call me," pouted Sherise, giving Emma a look of pure hatred before spinning away on her heels.

Calvin knew everyone there. Men stopped to shake his hand, others tapped him on the shoulder, women kissed him square on the lips. Once they had finally pushed their way through the mass of bodies, they found themselves in a hallway that led to wide open double-steel doors and, beyond that, like a window into another world, figures dancing in a cloud of smoke and lights.

The music was loud and intoxicating and Emma was caught up in the moment.

"Let's dance," she shouted above the noise.

"I don't dance." Then he touched the arm of a man standing by the door, whispered in his ear and gently propelled him in Emma's direction.

"Emma, Uncle Clayton, Uncle Clayton, Emma, go dance."

With that he walked off towards the bar, leaving her standing with the stranger.

Any worries that she'd be the oldest person there were quickly allayed by her new dance partner, Clayton.

Clayton must have been about 65 years old and what little was left of the fringe of curly hair that circled his crown was speckled grey. His skin, once stretched tight across his high, clearly-defined cheekbones was now softly-wrinkled and sagging, like a slowly deflating balloon a couple of days after the party is over.

But he was still in good shape, as was evident in the way his tight black pinstripe trousers and shiny red dress shirt clung to his body.

"Good evening ma'am," he smiled with a slight bow.

Not wanting to be impolite she smiled and let him lead the way to the dance floor.

Lucky for him – not so lucky for Emma – the music changed to a slow shuffle the minute they hit the dance floor. Clayton was in his element. He took her hand and, quite elegantly for a man of his height, held her waist, then led her through a series of complicated turns and quick steps which had her feet and her head spinning.

"Have you ever long-armed before?" he asked.

"Long-armed?"

"Yes, this, dancing with 'long arms', our version of ballroom."

"No," said Emma, laughing, "can't you tell?

She was amazed to see people of all ages, even the teenagers, grab a partner and twirl elegantly across the floor, switching from hip-hop to quick-step without, literally, skipping a beat.

He saw her look and said: "It's part of our culture, everyone knows how to long-arm. People see Coloureds and think all we're good for is stealing cars and doing drugs. They have no idea. My parents taught me to ballroom dance almost before I could walk, and I did the same with my kids."

"That's incredible."

Clayton was the kind of dancer who could make anyone look good, gently though expertly leading her across the dance floor, guiding her steps. Each time she faltered he caught her and put her on the right track and, by the time the music had ended, bumped off by another hard-hitting hip-hop number on the playlist, she was enjoying herself.

Slightly out of breath and laughing, Clayton led her to one of the tables ringing the dance floor and pulled out a seat for her.

"So Clayton, how do you know Calvin?" she asked once she'd caught her breath.

"His old man was my wife's brother, and one of my best friends growing up." Emma suddenly felt the atmosphere in the sweltering hall grow cold.

Seeming not to have noticed he went on: "We grew up on the same street, played together as lighties, always getting up to mischief," he chuckled at the memory. "We did our appy-ship on the railways together, only he quit after a year, I stayed on my whole life.

"Harry wanted something more from life," said Clayton, looking out onto the dance floor. "Wanted to be something, didn't want to lead the shit life he'd seen his mother and father and everyone else we knew lead. And he could have," he looked directly at her now. "Harry had it all: looks, talent, brains. If anyone could have made it out of here it was him. But in the end it pulled him back in."

Clayton grew quiet.

"Sorry my dear, still breaks me up to think of Harry. Now how do you know Calvin?"

"Oh, I'm a friend of Elizabeth."

"Good woman that, damn good woman," he said, sitting with his hands on his bony knees. "Saved Calvin's life, did you know that? Damn well saved his life. If it wasn't for that fine woman Calvin would have been on drugs or in jail or dead, like the others." And he shook his head sadly. "He should spend every breathing moment of his life thanking that woman for saving him, and I'm always telling him so. Been trying to get him to come to church with me for years, but he won't listen. Jesus, I tell him, he's the way and the life. I've tried to be there for the boy since the business with his father. But kids today, they got their own minds."

"What church do you belong to?"

"Catholic, my dear, like my parents and my parents' parents before them. There's also a Moslem side of the family," he said, "wear the head-scarves, pray to Allah, all of that. But I taught my children that Jesus was the answer, the only way."

Before it turned into a full-scale sermon Emma suggested they go get a drink and try to find Calvin.

They found him soon enough. Entangled in the arms of a stunning blonde along one particularly dark wall of the grimy bar.

Neither noticed Clayton and Emma standing there, and Clayton had to clear his throat before they paused to come up for air.

"Hey Uncle Clay, howzit," said Calvin good-naturedly, his arm still firmly around the blonde's waist, "did ya take Emma for a spin?"

"He's quite a dancer, your Uncle Clayton, you should have warned me," she said, giving him a significant look.

"Thought he might be able to teach ya a thing or two. Like Candy here is doin' for me," he said, jerking his head towards the blonde. She gazed adoringly at him. "Uncle Clay, Emma, meet Candy, she's as sweet as sugar," and she threw back her head and giggled breathlessly as he kissed her on her smooth, long neck.

"You the chick staying at the o' queen's cabin?" asked Candy and Emma was taken aback by her broad Coloured accent. She didn't know what she had expected but Candy was blonde and fair-skinned with brilliant blue eyes. She could have been plucked from the dark bar and placed in a pub in Scandinavia and not been one bit out of place.

But as she spoke it became obvious that her roots were no different to Clayton's or Calvin's, born and raised in Somerset or one of the suburbs like it.

"Yes, that's right."

"Calvin says you've joled from America."

"Yes."

"I'm joling to America, I'm a model you know. I want to become an actress...in Hollywood. Calvin tunes you can help."

Emma pierced Calvin with a look but he was too engrossed in Candy to notice.

"Well I'm not sure about that, I don't really know anyone in Hollywood."

"You don't?" she answered, wide-eyed. "You don't know any celebrities?"

"No," said Emma.

"Come on baby, no more praat 'bout America, I don't wanna think 'bout you leavin' me," said Calvin, his voice gravelly, and Candy, forgetting all thoughts of America, melted back into him.

Unable to stomach another round of impassioned kissing,

Emma suggested a dance and Clayton happily led her off.

"She wants to go to Hollywood? It's a crazy world, she wouldn't last a day!"

"Oh, I don't know," said Clayton, "she might. We're nothing, as a community, if not chameleons. We're all such a mixed bag it's just the luck of the draw how you turn out. Like dipping into a box of Smarties, it's that random." He had his hand on her elbow, gently leading her through the crowd towards the dance floor, his face close to hers so she could hear him above the noise. "You should see Coloured weddings, it's like the United Nations!" And he chuckled. "I know Candy's great grandmother on her father's side, she's a Black woman, lives in the rural areas, still carries water in a bucket from a river. But Candy got 'lucky', took after her Welsh great grandfather on her maternal side.

"You know what it all comes down to?" he said, not bothering to wait for an answer, "Hair."

"Hair?" asked Emma.

"Yes, hair," he said, pausing at the edge of the dance floor and turning to her. "What kind of hair you've got. Is it soft and straight like a White person's hair or tightly-curled or 'croos' as we call it. You ever heard of the 'pencil test'?"

"No, what on earth is that?" She had to shout to be heard over the music.

"In the old days they'd do the pencil test to see if you were pure White or had some mixed blood in you. Stick a pencil in your hair. If it fell out, you were safe, if it stayed in, tough luck. When I still had some, it was so croos I could keep the contents of a whole pencil case in my afro," said Clayton with a mock grimace, affectionately stroking his bald spot.

"That's bizarre," said Emma with a laugh.

"I've seen kids from around here, same mother, same father, one Whiter than you, the other dark as a Black man. I've seen families favour the fair child over the dark one, disown their Black relatives, pretend they're something they're not. But you can't run away from who you are forever, it has a funny way of catching up with you," he said, his voice suddenly sombre.

Then he took her hand and led her into the centre of the dance floor.

Emma and Clayton danced for over half an hour and, by the time they stopped, they were both flushed and perspiring. She'd enjoyed his company and thanked him for looking after her.

"My pleasure ma'am, always a pleasure to meet a true lady," he said, taking her hand. "I'd like to see you again Emma, no, no, nothing like that," he said when he saw her expression change, "I'm old enough to be your father. No, I'm going to tell Calvin to bring you round to meet my family, let's have Sunday lunch together. My wife makes a fantastic curry."

They made their way back to the bar and, although it was almost 2am, there was still no sign of the crowd thinning.

Calvin and Candy were exactly where they'd left them.

"Calvin, you planning to be here much longer? I think I'm ready to go."

"Nah, we can jol, ya ready to cut, baby?" He turned to Candy, his eyes hooded with desire. "Candy's jolin' cabin with us, I still have a lot to learn from her." And she just giggled again.

Before they said good-bye to Clayton they made arrangements for Sunday lunch, and then he kissed Emma's hand and started heading off into the darkness.

"Wait," Emma called after him, "don't you want a lift?"

"Thank you, ma'am, but I live just across the road, you can see my lounge window from a certain angle on the dance floor. That house," he said pointing into the dark road, "the one next door to the Mosque."

CHAPTER
EIGHTEEN

EMMA SLEPT IN late the following morning, exhausted and a little hung-over. When she woke up, the sun was already streaming through her curtains, flooding into the room with pink light.

When they got back to the house Calvin helped Candy out of the car, whispered something in her ear and slapped her on the butt as she'd walked toward the apartment, giggling.

He watched her leave then turned to Emma and smiled. "Had a lekker jol tonight?"

"Yes, I did, it was good fun. No thanks to you for deserting me."

"Ya a big girl, ya can look after yourself, that's wat ya tuned me. Besides, can you blame me?" And he looked longingly at Candy's retreating figure.

"I really can't comment. But you could have told me Clayton was Harry's best friend."

"Why, wat was gonna happen?"

"It was a little awkward, that's all. Did he know who I was?"

"Who gives a shit? Wat does he need to know that we don't know already? That ya an uptight White chick who needs to stop living in the past."

"Have you Calvin?"

"At least I've stopped dying in the present."

And with that he'd walked away towards his night of passion, leaving Emma alone and, once again, perplexed.

She'd woken to the sound of the shovel on the driveway again, and looked out of the window to see Calvin at work.

Emma washed, changed and went into the kitchen where a note from Elizabeth informed her she was out with a friend for the morning and that she should make herself at home.

She went outside and walked up to Calvin.

"Morning." The usual grunt in response. "So where's the lovely Candy this fine morning?"

"Joled cabin."

"Already?"

"Wat's she gonna chill here for? Unless she's planning to grab a shovel and graft. Speaking of which, there's a spare one back there." And he jerked his head towards the store room.

"No thanks. So, good night?"

A grunt.

"That's it?"

"It is wat it is, nothin' more, nothin' less. Enjoy it while it lasts. Ya should know." And he looked up and winked.

"Actually, no, I don't know. I don't see any man coming out of my bedroom this morning."

"And whose fault is that?"

"Whose fault?"

"I'm sure Uncle Clay would have been happy to oblige."

"Clayton's married!"

"Oh, jah, right, I forgot, and that'd be a big stress for ya." He stopped shovelling, picked up his discarded t-shirt with one hand and started wiping his brow with it. Then, leaning on the handle of the shovel, he looked directly at her. "I don't get ya."

"What do you mean?"

"Ya offering coffee again this morning? If you make me a cup I'll tune ya what I scheme. But I need to finish up here first."

Emma went in to make the coffee, her eyes inadvertently drifting to the picture on the pelmet. The thought went through her mind that if you could capture love in one moment, one brush stroke, it was there in her mother's eyes. It had somehow lived on in the picture when it had died in her.

Then she pushed all thoughts of her mother out of her mind and carried on making the coffee. Once it was ready she carried it onto the porch and called out to Calvin.

After a few minutes he joined her, wiping his brow with the t-shirt which he draped around his neck to protect it from the sun.

"Wat, no graze to jol with it?"

"You asked for coffee, not, as you so eloquently put it 'graze'."

"Shit, your o' man must have his hands full with ya!" he said, shaking his head. "Would have schemed by now he'd have taught ya a few things about an ouen: an ouen don't need to aks for graze, it should just jol. I scheme that's the trouble with hot chicks – like Candy, like you, probably ya o' queen, I don't know – you don't get wat an ouen needs," he said, spooning three heaped teaspoons of sugar into his coffee and stirring it.

"Oh really Calvin, well why don't you enlighten me?"

"Us ouens have simple needs – food, beer, sex. No praating, no nagging. Is that so hard for chicks to figure out?"

"OK, and now I'm going to give you a little home truth, something you may have missed while you were hiding out in your cave man dwelling," said Emma, putting down her coffee mug. "Times have changed, women are doing more, want more."

"Doin' more ouens, jah, ya got that right!" And he chuckled.

"You know that's not what I mean."

"So, Emma," and she was startled to hear him call her by her name, "what d' ya want that ya ain't got? Why ya tryin' to fill yourself with all sorts o' other shit?"

"I don't understand." Her voice had grown quiet.

"Wat ya doin' here? Wat you messing around behind your o' man's back for? Ya want more, I just don't scheme ya know wat ya want more of. Sex? Ya can get more sex anywhere, it's easy for chicks, especially good looking ones. Ya still hot. Is that wat ya want? I can hook you up." And he smiled as he put his lips to his coffee mug, squinting through the steam as he sipped.

"Shit, you know sometimes you drive me crazy!"

"Jah, baby, I know, that's what womens is always tunin' me." And he put down his mug and leaned back in the chair, fingers linked behind his head.

"No, Calvin, big surprise, it's not all about sex."

"I beg to differ," and he smiled, "but then ya'd have to have been there last night."

"And by this morning you've ditched her, so it couldn't have been enough."

"It was enough for then. And that makes it enough for me. That's where ya got it wrong, look for wat's enough for now, don't try and solve all the world's problems, ya'll never do it. Just drive ya mal in the head. Live for today, let tomorrow sort its own shit out."

"Do you think Candy feels the same way? Or, like that kid – Sherise – is she sitting by her phone waiting for you to call?"

"Don't know, don't care. She knew the deal and I didn't see no-one holding no gun to her head."

"So you don't feel guilty?"

"Guilty o' wat? I gave her a good time, aks her if ya see her, she'll tune you. Why, you feeling guilty? Ya wasting your time. Guilt's a wasted emotion."

"When did you become such a philosopher?"

"I'm no philosopher, just tune it like it is. So does he do it for ya?"

"Who?"

"Ya know who. Don't play dumb with me, it doesn't suit ya."

"Why do you think there's someone else?"

"Coz ya a fucking bad liar. And no-one's eyes light up when they answer the phone and it's their o' man on the line. Maybe, if they did, marriages would last longer. If the person we married could always get our blood hot. Is that it? Does he get your blood hot, Emma?" He was leaning forwards again, his eyes smoky slits.

"You said you wanted some food, let me go get us something to eat." And she started pushing herself off the chair.

"Nah, ya ain't going nowhere till ya tune me. You always duckin' and divin', just be straight for once."

"Why do you care so much anyway?" she said, sitting back down.

"I don't care, not as such. I'm just tired of the prissy, up-tight act. I know ya run piping hot under the surface, why ya so scared to show it?" he was looking intently at her. Her thoughts were swimming in the stare of his green eyes, drawing her in as had another pair – so startlingly similar – a long, long time ago.

Her voice was thin and breathless when she finally spoke. "Maybe because I've seen how it can destroy you and everyone around you."

"So ya'd rather live half a life? Ya'd rather live your life scared?"

"Don't we all?"

"Sut, not me. My days of being scared are over. Did enough of that as a lightie. So scared I was shittin' my bed till I was 12. My stepfather'd beat me bad and it'd only make me more scared, make me shit more. Nah, I ain't living my life like that no more," he said, shaking his head.

"What made you change?"

"Like I told ya, stop giving a shit, it won't change nothin' even if you do." Then as quickly as the intensity in his voice had come, it passed. He threw his arms over his head and stretched. "Now, where's that graze ya promised?"

CHAPTER
NINETEEN

AT BREAKFAST, CALVIN was back to his old self, the lid he'd lifted on his life so firmly back in place, Emma began to wonder if she'd imagined the emotion she'd glimpsed.

After eating a silent breakfast together, he went back to work and Emma didn't see much of him for the rest of the day. Elizabeth came home and they pottered around the house for a bit, then she pulled out her photo albums and they sat side-by-side in the sunlit lounge looking at pictures while the old woman reminisced about a life long-lost, children filling rooms now silently empty, birthday parties out on the front lawn, candles long since blown out.

The pictures reminded Emma of childhood pictures of her own, the same backdrop, different children. The difference was that all her photos ended when she was 10.

She couldn't help but think that there were no first day of high school pictures of her and Peter, no blushing teenage photos as they posed in their dress clothes before the leavers' dance. There were certainly no university graduation pictures, wedding shots and, saddest of all, no pictures of babies, no grandparents doting over grandchildren. And at that thought her heart pulled taut all over again.

The empty photo albums made her think of the emptiness of her life, the ghosts that inhabited her thoughts, often so much more life-like than the real people. And she thought again of Calvin's words: how was she trying to fill the emptiness?

Elizabeth sensed her mood and closed the photo albums, smiling kindly.

"Thank you my dear for pandering to the whims of a sad, lonely old woman hopelessly clinging to the past," she said, slowly standing up and taking the photo albums over to the book shelf by the fireplace. "I think that's quite enough, we have the present and future to focus on now, don't you think?" She put the albums away then turned back to look at Emma. "Well not so much me, but certainly you. Your whole life awaits you."

"It doesn't feel that way, sometimes it feels like I've seen the best of it…and it wasn't all that great."

"Nonsense, you're young, you're beautiful, you have so much to live for, to look forward to!" she said, walking back towards Emma, still sitting on the couch. "I suspect you've gone your whole life not seeing all you have within you as clearly as those around you do."

"It's just so hard," she said, looking up at the old woman, and her voice threatened to be washed away by a rush of emotion she was only just managing to hold back.

"Of course it is, dear, nothing worth having is easy."

"I'm so confused I'm even thinking of taking Calvin's advice," and she laughed sadly.

"And what's that?"

"Stop caring, just stop caring. Then, somehow, it won't hurt so much anymore."

"Huh, is that what he told you? That boy's a rascal." But as she said it she was smiling with affection. "And a liar by the way! Stop caring? If only he could. Now I'm going to tell you a story which you must never tell a soul, certainly not Calvin," she said, sitting back down next to Emma, taking her hand and looking intently at her. "He'd kill me if he knew I'd told you, it might damage his big macho image and God knows we would never want that! I don't normally break a confidence but I think, in this case, it's one that needs to be broken."

CHAPTER TWENTY

ABOUT FIVE YEARS after Calvin moved in with them, said Elizabeth, they began to notice there was something wrong with him. Not so much emotionally, although Elizabeth had always suspected there were wounds there so deep that, if opened, he would likely bleed to death.

No, it was physical. He was in his early 20s, at the peak of his fitness, always working, running, exercising for hours in the apartment, long after everyone else had gone to bed.

But suddenly he seemed to be perpetually tired and worn-out, as if he had a leak and all the life in him was slowly draining away.

He couldn't seem to get up in the mornings and, when he eventually did, he would drag himself around like an old man.

"It was an awful sight to see," said Elizabeth, bringing her hands up to cover her cheeks, a shadow falling over her eyes.

Elizabeth paid him special attention, made him all his favourite foods, hoping to nourish him back to energy and strength. But nothing worked.

Finally she persuaded him to let her take him to the family doctor. He went into the surgery alone and was in there for a full 45 minutes. When he came out he was as reticent as always and, although she pried gently, he told her very little except that the doctor had asked a lot of questions and given him a Vitamin B injection.

The doctor called Elizabeth in the next day, saying there was something he wanted to discuss with her.

She stepped into his surgery with a feeling of dread. He closed the door behind her and indicated for her to take a seat, sitting opposite her at his desk.

Then he rested his elbows on the desk and interlaced his hands under his chin, sitting silently pensive for a few minutes before proceeding.

"Elizabeth," he said and he pursed his lips, "I'm not really sure where to start." Dr Hodges had been their family doctor for years, knew their family intimately.

"Have you noticed any unusual behaviour in Calvin, besides the fatigue you mentioned before you brought him in?"

"No, none really that I can say, besides the fatigue and lack of energy. Calvin, as you know, doesn't live in the house with us, he's in the apartment and more or less does his own thing. Why, John? You're making me anxious," and she leaned forward in her seat.

She watched the bushy overhang of his eyebrows knit in a frown. "So you don't really monitor the hours he keeps, that sort of thing?"

"No, he's old enough to come and go as he pleases. I'm not his jailer, I'm more like his landlady. Besides, he's independent, not the kind of boy to take kindly to restraint."

"So you wouldn't be aware that he has not slept a single night at the house for the last two months?"

"No I wouldn't. John, what's happened, is it a woman? Oh Lord, he hasn't caught some dreadful disease has he?" she said, wringing her hands together in her lap. "He is a bit of a ladies' man, that I have to admit."

"No Elizabeth, nothing like that. When I've finished telling you the story maybe you'll be able to understand."

It had taken a great deal of persuasion before Calvin opened up and told Dr Hodges his story and it was a testament to the doctor's perseverance that he hadn't given up during the first 10 minutes of Calvin's stubborn silence.

Eventually it had taken a threat that he would recommend Elizabeth give him notice to leave the apartment if he didn't tell him what was going on that persuaded him to talk, slowly at first and then in an endless rush.

CHAPTER
TWENTY-ONE

Calvin 1980

WEDNESDAY NIGHTS WERE the worst. Wednesdays were half-price night at the Legion Club and Uncle Kevin was always the first one there, just as the club opened its doors at 5. By 9.30 he'd be completely tanked, teetering his way home, usually in a foul mood. Uncle Kevin was an ugly drunk.

'Uncle Kevin' had been the way Calvin's mother had introduced him to the children the first time he came to the apartment.

It was no formal introduction.

"Jol and get Uncle Kevin a beer." He was short and rake thin, with straight, pitch-black hair, not much darker than his skin colour, and small, red eyes.

He didn't say a single word to them that first day. He and Gwennie sat on the cramped balcony talking and drinking beer until way after sunset, Gwennie's high-pitched laughter drifting on the lazy afternoon from the second floor apartment down to the dusty courtyard below where the children played.

Calvin and Bernice were in charge of getting the beers, two at a time so they wouldn't get warm, running fast up the steps when they heard their mother call, careful not to take too long and make her mad. Talia was a baby then, just learning to walk. When she took her first tentative steps, frantically stretching her chubby arms from one armchair to the next then stumbling unsteadily forward, Harry was already gone. He never saw his little girl's first steps. Mind you, neither did Gwennie. She'd been on night shift. Or at the Club. Calvin couldn't remember which. Either way, he and Bernice were baby-sitting when Talia started walking.

When the sun sank behind the apartment block and the shadows lengthened across the courtyard, the children went inside.

Talia was getting hungry and starting to niggle. Her face was smeared with mud, her chubby hands holding fistfuls of sand, embedded in her fingernails, tucked deep in the creases of the baby fat around her neck and thighs.

Bernice was small for seven and struggled to grab Talia's round drenched bottom and carry her.

Calvin ran on ahead, hearing another summons from Gwennie for beer.

When he went upstairs the house was dark. Gwennie and Uncle Kevin were no longer on the balcony and Calvin was instructed to leave the beers by the bedroom door.

He did as he was told and then wandered into the kitchen to see what there was to eat. A greasy frying pan topped the pile of dirty dishes by the sink and flies hovered over a stale piece of bread on the floor.

Calvin walked to his mother's bedroom door and called "Ma, what's for dinner?" But no-one replied. He knocked but, still, no-one answered.

"Where's Ma?" asked Bernice, panting as she deposited a crying Talia on the floor.

"Dunno."

Bernice made to go into the room but Calvin grabbed her arm and pulled her back.

"You know Ma tunes we must never go into her room unless she tunes us we can."

"But I'm hungry!" Bernice was whining. Talia's wailing was beginning to work on her nerves.

"I'll get us some graze."

Calvin went back into the kitchen and opened the fridge. Besides beers there wasn't much in it. Half a jug of milk, a block of margarine, half a dozen eggs.

He looked for a pan he could use but they were all dirty, piled high in the sink. Finally, right at the back of the cupboard, he found a small rusted frying pan with a crooked base that wobbled noisily when he placed it on the greasy stove plate.

Next he found oil, pouring what was meant to be just a drop but, through a sudden jerk of his unsteady hand, became half a pan full.

He turned on the stove and waited for the oil to bubble and pop. Then he took three eggs from the fridge and cracked them clumsily on the side of the counter, streaks of glistening egg white connecting the counter to the pan like silver-spun spider webs as he hastily dropped them in, tossing the crumpled shells to one side.

Talia had wandered into the kitchen and was tugging on his shorts, crying to be picked up.

"Bernice, come get Talia, I'm busy!"

But Bernice was in the toilet and didn't hear him.

Talia's cries were getting louder and she was tugging hard.

"Wait Talia, wait! I'm trying to cook, wat you doing?"

Calvin was holding the handle of the pan with one hand, trying to prise Talia's grubby fingers off his shorts with the other. The base was wobbling badly and the oil was bouncing off in hissing bubbles.

Then all of a sudden the bubbles erupted and began to spit angrily at him, stinging his hand in a thousand different places. He jumped, splashing hot oil out of the pan. Onto the floor around him. Onto Talia.

Ever seen the rivers that cut through a bowl of flour when you add oil to it? That was all his scarred mind could register as he watched the oil run rivulets through the right side of his baby sister's face. That was all he could think as her howl of pain rose from the floor and washed over him. That was all he could think as his mother came running into the kitchen, hair wild, gown flapping open to reveal a pair of pendulous breasts.

Bernice was right behind her, screaming, and, in the background, Uncle Kevin, hands on his head, running aimlessly back and forth.

In one corner of his shocked mind Calvin was wondering why Uncle Kevin was wearing his father's boxer shorts.

CHAPTER
TWENTY-TWO

THE NEXT DAY Uncle Kevin visited again and this time he did speak to them.

"Get me a beer, boy!" His dark jowls were shaded with stubble and Calvin noticed for the first time that one of his front teeth was missing.

Gwennie had spent the night at the hospital with Talia and Uncle Kevin had come to the apartment to wait for her.

"Did you see Talia?" Calvin asked, having had no news of her or his mother since the ambulance came to take them to the hospital the previous night.

"Wat?"

"Did you see my sister?"

"Sut." No. And that was that.

Day three passed much the same. Gwennie's sister, Joobie, came to babysit the children but still had no details about Talia, no reassurances for Calvin.

Uncle Kevin came again and increased his communication to him by one word. "Get me a cold beer, boy!"

Gwennie and Talia came home on the fourth day. By then Uncle Kevin was firmly ensconced in what had mysteriously become "his spot", the wing-back chair in the corner facing the TV, the one which would have been the only posh piece of furniture in the apartment if the upholstery wasn't coming away in long, ragged threads, unravelling itself from the arms outwards.

Talia had fallen asleep in the taxi and Gwennie carried her in her arms. Calvin stood up on tip-toe to see her but his mother pushed him impatiently away. All he could see was the top of her head, swathed in bandages and seeping thick yellow ointment. He felt his stomach turn.

From that day on Uncle Kevin never left. He took up firm residence in two spots in the cramped one bedroom apartment: on the armchair and in Gwennie's bed. His days were spent forming one endless trail from the lounge to the bedroom, showing little inclination to venture any further. A dank, unwashed smell followed Uncle Kevin's looping trail.

For several weeks after the accident Talia slept in the room with Uncle Kevin and Gwennie but, as she slowly began to heal, the blisters turning from raw flesh to rubbery scar, she was sent back to the lounge to sleep with Calvin and Bernice.

The children had to wait for Uncle Kevin to switch off the TV and go to bed before they could roll out the mattresses and go to sleep. Sometimes, on school nights, they would try to sleep through the noise of the TV. It worked on most nights except Wednesday, Uncle Kevin's big night out. On those nights, even if they were already asleep when he finally rolled in, he would switch the TV on full blast and sit belching and swearing in the armchair until the early hours of the morning.

Talia's scars, running from her smooth round forehead, down the side of her face and into her hairline, were Calvin's constant reminder of the accident. Gwennie was the other. She never missed an opportunity to reprimand him for his carelessness, finding fault in almost everything he did, pointing out Talia's scars to anyone and everyone and apportioning blame.

Before long Uncle Kevin had jumped on the bandwagon, making Calvin his personal punching bag.

They were married six months after Talia's accident, in a cold, grey magistrate's court one icy June afternoon. Uncle Kevin wore an ill-fitting pin-striped suit which sagged at the shoulders, Gwennie clutched a bouquet of artificial flowers as her only concession to bridal wear. Other than that she was plainly dressed in a brown polyester trouser suit, flat brown sandals on her long, thin feet.

That night – the honeymoon night – Uncle Kevin was in a particularly festive mood. He and Gwennie sat drinking on the porch long after the handful of guests invited to celebrate the nuptials had left. When Gwennie finally went to bed, he slumped in his armchair and cranked up the volume on the crackling old black and white TV, laughing and singing to himself.

The children had been fast asleep when the noise jolted them awake. Calvin looked up, bleary-eyed, and saw Uncle Kevin washed a deathly grey by the eerie glow of the TV screen.

"Wat d'ya want boy?" he said when he saw Calvin looking at him. Then he nudged him sharply with the toe of his boot and ordered him to bring him a beer.

Calvin stood up unsteadily and walked, dazed and half asleep, to the kitchen, bringing back a beer.

"From now on, boy," he slurred, grabbing the beer from his hand, "you'll call me Dad."

That was the night Calvin started wetting his bed.

CHAPTER
TWENTY-THREE

TALIA HAD A pretty face, but the first thing people noticed was not the almost perfectly round shape of it, her deep-set hazel-coloured eyes, so much like Harry's. It was the burn marks which, as she grew, settled into a deep mulberry-coloured stain. Her saving grace was her hair, long, wavy and jet black, which, when loose, covered much of the scar. Her other disguise was her hand. She'd cross her left arm over her chubby waist, rest the right elbow on it and tilt her head to the right side, face cupped in her hand like she was pondering something or was very tired. It became such a habit, she didn't know she was doing it.

One day, when she was six, she came home from school in tears. Gwennie was at work, Uncle Kevin was asleep, snoring loudly in the armchair, and only Calvin was home and awake.

He was playing football in the courtyard, kicking up dust that swirled around him like a whirlwind, spinning agilely in the centre of it, the ball stuck, as if by glue, to the toe of his shoe as he deftly manoeuvred it up and down.

He stopped when he saw Talia coming around the corner, dragging her school bag on the ground, the belt of her blue and white striped school uniform dangling, her hair sticking in thick, damp streaks to her face.

Her quiet tears, contained for so long, escalated to loud sobs the minute she saw him, and she dropped her school bag and ran towards him, burying her face in his belly.

"Hey Talia, why you crying?" Then his voice turned suddenly harsh, "Was someone bullying ya? Who Talia, who was it? Tell me and I'll gun 'em!"

"No," she said through the tears. Calvin was awkwardly tapping the top of her head. "My teacher…" and a fresh flood of sobs drowned out the rest of the sentence.

"Your teacher wat? Wat did your teacher do? Talia, I can't help ya if ya don't tune me wat went down."

He gently led her to the steps of the building, her face never leaving the safety of his belly, and sat her down beside him.

Worn out and breathless from the sobbing, taking in great gulps of air in between the words, she managed to tell him what happened.

"Mrs Drake, she called me stupid and the whole class laughed."

"Why did she call you stupid?"

"Coz I can't write proper."

"What d'ya mean? Ya write good! Ya always writing at cabin."

"Coz I can't write proper with the other hand."

"The other hand?" He was frowning.

"I can't write proper with this hand," she said raising her chubby left hand, the tiny square palm smeared with a mixture of

140

mud and tears.

"But ya don't write with ya left hand."

"I do at school." Her voice was a tiny whisper.

"Why?"

"Coz I do."

And then it hit him.

"Chill here, I'm joling upstairs."

He was back a moment later, an exercise book and a pen in his hand. He handed them to Talia and instructed her to write like she did at school.

She automatically picked the pen up in her right hand and started writing.

"No, Talia, like you do at school."

She looked up at him almost guiltily and swapped hands. Then she leaned her elbow on the book, rested her face in it and started writing with her left hand. The words were nothing but scribbles.

"Why d'ya use that hand at school?" he asked, even though he already knew the answer.

"They all laugh," was all she said, her voice shaking.

And Calvin felt the pain like a kick in the gut.

"Ya tell 'em they better not laugh or ya big bro's gonna come and pump 'em up, ok? Ya fucking tune 'em!"

Talia clapped her hand over her mouth. "Calvin, you said a swear word!"

"I'm 12 Talia, I'm allowed."

"Mommy will be mad."

"Why? She says it all the time. Ya allowed to when ya a grown up. Ya can't coz ya still a lightie, but Mommy and me, we're big.

So tune 'em ok? Tune 'em wat I'll do to 'em if they laugh. And you gotta start writing with your proper hand Talia, how else you gonna learn anything at school?"

"I don't wanna go to school no more." Her full lips were turned down, her shoulders slumped.

"Don't never say that, Tal, you gotta go to school. You gotta learn stuff."

"Why? I don't wanna!" She folded her chubby arms over her chest and pouted.

"So you can become something."

"I am something, I'm a girl."

"I mean something that gives you sheets, money. Ya need to jol to school for that. Then ya won't need to have a hard life like Ma, you can live in a lekker cabin and have wheels of ya own. Wouldn't that be lekker, to drive ya kids to school? Then they don't have to get wet when it's raining and get to school all sopping wet with socks squishy in their shoes like we do," said Calvin, holding one foot in the air and pointing to it. "That's what sheets does, Talia, it buys ya lekker items."

"Like what?"

"A lekker cabin, wheels, oh never mind, ya too little to understand. Jol upstairs and change out of ya school uniform and ya can come play football with me."

Talia whooped with delight, all her sadness forgotten, bouncing her bag up the steps behind her as she ran upstairs.

CHAPTER
TWENTY-FOUR

BY THE TIME Calvin left home, Gwennie and Kevin's marriage, never on firm ground, was in turmoil. They would have separated long ago but Kevin wouldn't move out.

The fighting was continuous and had reached an ugly new level of violence. It was worse after they'd been drinking which they both did more and more as the home situation spiralled.

The fights were usually about money, but could be about any number of things. By the time the slapping and kicking had begun, they'd forgotten exactly what they'd started fighting about in the first place.

Gwennie could throw the punches as well as she could take them, and many mornings Kevin would be the one who rolled out of bed with a black eye.

The fighting would start early in the morning and carry on well into the night, long after the children had gone to bed.

Sometimes it would be so bad the neighbours would shout for them to shut up, but Gwennie would just turn more abusive.

"This is my cabin and I can shout as loud as I fuckin' want!"

she would rant out of the window back at them. "Don't act like ya shit Ponds, Doris Lambert! D'ya think no-one knows ya fuckin' ya sister's o' man and you tell me to shut up? Fuck off, all of ya!" At moments like these Calvin would watch his mother, hair wild, face streaked with venom, and wonder whether she really had gone mad.

Kevin now took to sleeping permanently on the armchair in the lounge and, from this vantage point, could more easily bully and torment the children, Calvin his prime target. The first time he'd slapped Calvin across the back of his head it had been tentative, waiting for a protest from Gwennie. When none came, he continued.

The slaps became harder and more intense and there was rarely any reason for them. They became like punctuation in his speech. The exclamation mark at the end of a sentence. The question mark after an enquiry. He was always more vicious towards Calvin after he'd received a particularly good beating from Gwennie.

Gwennie had changed completely after Harry had gone. Not that he'd been around much towards the end anyway.

"Always fuckin' graftin'," she'd sometimes spit in his face as he walked out the door before sunrise some days, getting home long after dark.

She'd never been the maternal type. If the children hurt themselves it was Harry they'd run to, Harry who would kiss and hug them hello in the mornings and call "love you" after them as they ran out the door to school.

Open affection was just something Gwennie was never very good at. She reminded Calvin a lot of his grandmother, a tough, wiry old woman who, at 78, could still drink and swear with the best of them.

Gwennie would watch Harry's easy affection with a mixture of puzzlement and envy. She'd reprimand him for "being too soft on the lighties" but there was a longing in her eyes for the kind of open love he could show and which remained so tightly locked inside her.

When Calvin and Bernice were little she would show her love in other ways: making pretty dresses for Bernice, mending Calvin's beloved football.

She was house-proud then. The apartment they lived in at the time was as small and cramped as this one, but it was always clean and tidy, the floors polished until they shone, starched, white lace mats on the smooth, dark wooden coffee table and the old record player in the corner. The sprigs of artificial flowers set in a fake crystal vase were always carefully dusted, the florist wires that held them in place straightened and stretched into shape.

Gwennie was never a great cook but she had her specialities, her tried and tested favourites. Calvin remembered her hearty beef stews in winter, the gravy thick and rich. Or her spaghetti bolognaise, the sauce made with little meatballs, each one individually fried to perfection.

Once Harry was gone the part of her which had slowly started to wilt towards the end of their relationship, seemed to shrivel up and die altogether.

She had shrugged on a hard coat over her already tough exterior and nothing seemed to penetrate it. She lost interest in the home, in cooking, in the children, in herself. Her hair had always been coarse and dry but, in the early days, she'd taken the time to give it regular oil treatments and style it. After Harry, all that extra care she'd give to her hair fell away and she left it to become a frizzy, unkempt halo surrounding her head. She rarely wore any make up and even stopped using the sweet rose-scented hand lotion Calvin had always associated with his mother. Her skin had become dry and lined, and there were dark smudges under her eyes.

Calvin couldn't remember the last time his mother had helped him with his homework, said one word that wasn't either insult, reprimand or command, or cooked them a proper meal. It was like she'd checked out of motherhood early.

It had been manageable before Uncle Kevin arrived. But when his slaps progressed to punches and kicks and, still, Gwennie didn't step in and help him, Calvin realised he was on his own.

By the time he was 17 he was a head taller than Kevin, broad-chested and handsome, features so similar to Harry they haunted Gwennie and she found herself, towards the end, hardly able to look at him at all. Calvin interpreted her avoidance as lack of love and withdrew further.

Despite his strength he had never fought back, never challenged Kevin, tried not to rock the boat. But the storm inside him was brewing.

He left home on a Thursday morning. He remembered it clearly because Kevin had come in late as usual from half-price Wednesday. Instead of heading for the armchair to pick an argument with the children before falling into a loud snoring heap, he'd rolled noisily towards Gwennie's bedroom and thrown open the door.

Calvin could hear muffled angry noises and Kevin's voice getting loud and insistent.

He was full of alcoholic strength and courage and, taking Gwennie by surprise in her sleep, had, for once, easily overpowered her.

Calvin knew the golden rule: never go into his mother's bedroom unless she explicitly gave him permission. But when Gwennie's shouts went from an angry yell to a painful howl, a sound like an animal in danger that he'd never heard his fearless mother make, he stormed in.

Gwennie was lying on her back and Kevin had pinned both her wrists over her head with one hand. With the other hand he had torn open her night gown and was clutching her throat. Kevin had taken one too many barbs about his relationship with Gwennie in the club, one too many insinuations about his lack of manhood. Tonight he was going to have her, and no-one was going to stop him.

They both looked around, startled, when Calvin flew in and, with one swift, smooth movement plucked Kevin off the bed as easily as flicking a cockroach off a curtain. He lay on the ground, Calvin looming over him, fists poised. Kevin, suddenly sober, was wide-eyed and shaking, his hands raised protectively over his face.

And then Gwennie did a curious thing.

"Calvin, get out," her voice was low but insistent.

"Wat?" he couldn't believe what he was hearing, "No! I'm gonna kill this fucker!"

"No ya not!" her voice was rising. "Get out! Just get out, I can handle it! Go!"

Kevin took in the scene and smirked. He got up off the floor and lunged murderously towards Calvin who, shocked and defeated, just stood and took the searing blow to his head.

"I said get out!" shrieked Gwennie as Kevin removed a switchblade from his pocket and came towards him.

Calvin, seeing Gwennie's panicked look but still not fully understanding it, left the room, left the apartment.

Kevin's taunting abuse followed him all the way out of the courtyard and into the street beyond. It was 1am and all he had were the clothes he was wearing and the letter. And now he knew where he would go.

CHAPTER
TWENTY-FIVE

CALVIN WASN'T SURE what he expected to find at number 17, wasn't sure he'd find what he needed to make everything that had seemed so wrong in his life for so long right. All he had was the letter, tucked deep into an inner pocket of a tan jacket his mother had given him when he'd grown out of his own.

"Here, take this!" She'd flung it at him one morning as the weather had stormed overnight into a cold, wet day. "Ya fuckin' father ain't gonna be needin' it no more."

He'd shrugged it on and it fitted him perfectly. Gwennie had looked away.

About a month later, searching his pockets for a box of matches to light his cigarette, he opened the zip to one of the inside pockets and felt something crisp lying at the bottom. He pulled out the single sheet of thin paper, folded in half and then half again.

He must have read the seven lines, written in a neat woman's hand-writing, more than 50 times. He had memorised every word, every slant of every character. And now he was treading determinedly towards the address written in the top right hand corner.

The middle-aged woman who walked to the gate when he rang the cow bell was hesitant but kind. He had looked a real sight. He hadn't slept all night, hadn't eaten for 24 hours. He was wearing the track suit bottoms and vest he normally slept in and trainers without socks. His eyes were darting red slits.

"Yes?"

"I'm looking for David Hardy," he said.

"No, there's no David Hardy here," she said. "We bought the house from his estate."

"He's dead?"

"Yes, some years ago. Why, young man, why did you want to see him?"

"My old man worked for him." And now she could see the carefully tucked away emotion swimming in his green gaze.

"Who was your father?"

"Harry Rhoades." His voice turned hoarse as he said his name.

Elizabeth had followed the case closely in the press and knew exactly who Harry Rhoades was. Calvin could see the glint of recognition in her eyes.

"Sorry, young man, we can't help you."

Then, on impulse and because he had nowhere else to turn, he asked if there was any work for him.

For years afterwards he would wonder why, knowing who he was, she hadn't sent him away right there and then but, instead, had looked at him long and hard and, as if she had made up her mind, told him to come back at 5 when her husband would be home from work. She started to walk back down the long driveway but, almost as if on instinct, turned around and asked him if he was hungry.

"No ma'am." She sensed his stubborn pride.

"It's just that I made a cake and my children don't like it much, I don't want to see it going to waste. You'll be doing me a favour by eating it."

He shrugged, and she smiled. She went back to the house, returning with a slice of banana cake the size of a doorstop.

Calvin reached out and took it from her with a gruff thank you, then sat down on the culvert. He was ravenous and barely managed to resist the urge to stuff it into his mouth, restraining himself until she had walked back down the driveway and disappeared, out of sight, into the house. Then he ate it feverishly, almost without swallowing, and, when it was all gone, sat quietly catching his breath.

He waited on the culvert until 5 when a blue Peugeot 505 pulled up at the gate and a balding, middle-aged man stepped out. He wasn't surprised to see Calvin sitting there, his wife had phoned him at the office and told him about the young man who had pitched up at the gate.

At first James had been reluctant to take on the Coloured boy, but Elizabeth had begged him to think about it.

"There's just something about him, James. I can't quite put my finger on it, but I think we should help him."

"But his father..."

"More reason to give him a chance. You and I always agreed Harry Rhoades got a raw deal, the cards were stacked against him before he even began. This may be our chance to right the wrong."

Her husband had learnt over the years that Elizabeth's instincts were rarely wrong and, besides, they could use a handy-man on the property.

Still, when Calvin leapt to his feet as James Calderwood pulled up at the gate, he was a little taken aback by his appearance and wavered. Until he saw Elizabeth waving cheerfully to him from the porch, her face beaming, and he remembered how few things his wife ever asked of him.

He told Calvin to follow him inside and wait on the porch. Then he parked the car and went in to put down his briefcase and jacket before coming out to speak to him.

Calvin was standing to one side, his hands clasped nervously behind his back. James told him to sit down and gestured to a garden chair, taking the one opposite him.

"What is it you want us to do for you...Calvin, is it?" said James, sitting back in his chair and crossing his legs as he observed the young man sitting opposite him.

"I need a graft – a job – sir, and a place to stay."

"Where have you been staying all this time?"

"With my mother."

"And?"

"There was a span of us in the house, decided it was time to leave and find graft," he said.

"A sudden decision was it?" he said, looking at his clothes, his lack of luggage.

"Yes sir."

"OK. And what kind of work can you do?"

"I can do anything sir. I'm strong and I'm good with my hands. I did Design and Technology at school…and I passed," and there was pride in his voice. "Ya wouldn't need to pay me, if ya give me a place to stay I'll do any graft ya need for free. When ya don't need me I'll find other graft in the area."

"Hmm, it's an interesting proposition Calvin, but you realise the risk is all ours?" said James, pushing his glasses up the bridge of his nose. I don't know you, not as a person, not as a worker, I have no idea what you're capable of. I'll tell you what, let's try things out for two weeks and see how it goes. If we're happy with each other you can stay on, if not we'll ask you to leave. Deal?"

"Deal."

It didn't take long for Calvin to prove himself in his work. It took him even less time than that to work his way into Elizabeth's affections.

Soon after he had moved into the room at the back, Elizabeth went to the library at the local daily newspaper and looked up the files on Harry.

Sure enough Calvin was mentioned in the reports, along with two younger sisters and a wife, Gwennyth Rhoades. There was even a grainy photograph in one of the newspaper cuttings of the family and, looking at the picture, she realised with a start how much of that scrawny, scared little boy still lived in the 17 year old Calvin.

Her heart went out to him all over again.

Elizabeth's family had always said she was a soft touch, and never softer than when it came to Calvin.

James and the two children grew fond of him too, but never to the same extent as Elizabeth.

Her eldest son, Steve, would tease her that Calvin was her favourite son.

"Well with you and your brother always gadding about, he'll probably be the one to stick around and look after me when I'm old and decrepit," she'd say.

Calvin kept to himself much of the time and Elizabeth didn't like to interfere. But about four years after he moved in with them he came to the kitchen door and, as was his habit, tapped softly on the door then stepped back and stood to one side, waiting for someone to come.

Elizabeth had been in the kitchen cooking and very quickly answered his knock at the door.

"Yes, dear?" said Elizabeth, drying her hands on a tea towel.

"I've had a message from my o' que – my mother," he looked down at his feet. "She's asked me to go see her. I may be gone a day or two."

"Your mother? Is everything alright dear?"

"Dunno ma'am, that's why I gotta go. Will you please say sorry to Mr Calderwood and tell him I'll finish the shelves in the workshop soon as I get back?"

"Don't worry about that, dear, just go along to your mother and make sure everything is OK."

He thanked her and hurried up the driveway.

Elizabeth was perplexed. Calvin had never spoken about his family and the one time she had asked him how his mother was doing he had visibly frozen, then muttered something about not seeing her much. Elizabeth had been concerned that his work schedule was keeping him from visiting his family but, when she suggested he take some time off to go see them, he politely but firmly cut her off, saying there was no need.

Calvin was gone for two days and returned to work without a word. Elizabeth hadn't wanted to press him. But from then on, at least once a month, he would announce that he was going to spend the night with his family and would be gone for two days.

Then a year later, the sickness began.

CHAPTER
TWENTY-SIX

WHEN CALVIN RECEIVED the note from his mother, his stomach clenched into a tight knot. It didn't say much, just three lines in Gwennie's sketchy though familiar hand writing.

Calvin,

Kevin's gone. Talia's in trouble. I need to see you.

Mom

Again that icy cold shudder of guilt as he thought of Talia's face.

Calvin stood by the side of the road and flagged down a mini bus taxi bound for town. He sat in the back row, sandwiched between a young mother and her crying baby and an old man smelling strongly of wood smoke and sweat.

He was so pre-occupied he missed his stop, and had to get down at 20th Avenue and back-track the three blocks to the apartment.

He rounded the corner with dread, passing a dusty auction centre on one side, an office stationery supplier on the other, and turned into the familiar alleyway leading to the apartment building.

As he passed through the wide gates and entered the square courtyard, his footsteps faltered. His last memory was walking through here in the early hours of the morning, the moon still up, the air carrying a pre-dawn chill. His chest visibly heaving through his thin vest.

He remembered the effort it took to contain his fear, his shock, his rage. He remembered with shame the hot, angry tears which had coursed down his face and the ache in his chest as he thought of leaving behind his sisters and, as cold and distant as she had become over the years, his mother.

Despite everything this had been home. Once this had been all he'd known.

He was returning a completely different person, a stranger. At times even to himself.

There was a figure standing under the stairs leading up to the apartment and, as he drew closer, he recognised it as Bernice.

The first thought that went through his mind was how tall she'd grown, the second was that she was standing with a man and smoking a cigarette.

Calvin's mind reeled and he instinctively quickened his step, ready to grab the cigarette out of her mouth and crush it under his shoe. Until he remembered she wasn't alone. And she was no longer his little sister.

She heard his footsteps and swung her head around, her hair flying across her face. My God, she's gorgeous, he thought to himself. And she was.

Bernice, always rake-thin and bony, had grown slender and willowy. Her waist was pinched in, her hips curvaceous. She was lovely and sensual…and she knew it.

A shadow of doubt passed over her face when she caught sight of Calvin, then immediately transformed into pure delight.

"Calvin! Calvin it's you! Calvin!"

She was shrieking his name, running towards him, her arms outstretched. She flung them around his neck and held on tightly as he swung her off her feet.

"Hey little 'ster, wat's happening?"

Then he put her down and held her at arm's length so he could take a better look at her. He wanted to tell her how beautiful she was, but his voice caught in his throat and all he said was "Shit you've grown!"

"I know, look, I've got boobs!" she said, cupping her breasts with her hands, her cheeks flushed with pleasure.

"You call those boobs?" he laughed along with her.

The man she'd been talking to was hanging awkwardly back in the shadows, and now Calvin pierced him with a look which stopped Bernice in mid-giggle.

"Tyrone, come here and meet my big bro."

He tried to look casual, but it wasn't working.

"Calvin," said Tyrone, nodding his head slightly in his direction and putting out his hand to perform the intricate greeting that had taken the place of shaking hands.

Calvin jutted his chin upwards, ignoring the outstretched hand. "'Sup?"

"Come on, let's go upstairs, Talia's gonna freak out when she sees you!" Bernice caught him by the arm and started pulling him upstairs, leaving Tyrone standing there on his own.

Glancing back she called to him, "Later Ty, I'm busy with my bro now."

And Calvin took pleasure in seeing the resentment on his face as he watched them leave.

"Who's the asshole?"

"What asshole?" said Bernice. "He's my boyfriend," and she bubbled with raucous laughter.

"Boyfriend? Since when did you start having dudes?"

"Where you been, Calvin? I've had boyfriends for years. Even Talia has a boyfriend."

"Wat? Ya gotta be kidding me!"

"Aks her yourself," she said with a mischievous grin.

He had to run to keep up with her, noticing out of the corner of his eye that nothing much had changed. The paint was still peeling, the dust still sat in tunnels along each step. A discarded chip packet bounced down the stairs past them and the sound of music coming from number three was still as loud and thumping as he remembered. His mind was tossed back to weekday evenings when they'd be trying to finish off their homework and get ready for bed with that incessant blare, so loud it was as if it was being played right there in the lounge with them.

Bernice flung open the door of the tiny apartment and yelled "He's home! Calvin's home!" Her announcement was met by a scream as Talia came tearing out of the kitchen.

She too flung herself at Calvin and held him tight, burying her face in his shoulder.

When she lifted her head he saw her eyes were brim-full of tears only barely held back by her long eye-lashes. As she stood looking at him one escaped, falling from her dark lash down onto her cheek.

Calvin reached up with one finger and wiped the tear away, staring into the eyes of his baby sister, doing all he could to avoid looking at her scar.

She wasn't as tall as Bernice and was still fairly plump, her jeans stretched tight across her belly and chubby thighs. Her t-shirt bulged a little over her waist and she had quite a large bust but she still had that captivating look of innocent beauty that she'd had as a little girl. Her wide, almond-shaped eyes shone with life and light and her hair, always so sleek and glossy, fell in waves around her oval face.

He was silent for a few moments, not knowing what to say or do. Then he kissed Talia on the forehead, just at the point where her scars began and said, "Howzit, Tal."

"You came." The three of them turned to see Gwennie standing in the doorway of her bedroom, three in the afternoon and still wearing her dressing gown. Her hair was unruly and her eyes smudged with sleeplessness; Calvin noticed how much she'd aged in the time he'd been away.

"Hey Ma," he said, hesitant, not sure whether to step forward and hug her or not. When she made no move towards him he held back but he couldn't help but see a dim light awaken in her dark eyes.

Then Gwennie went back into the bedroom, gesturing for Calvin to follow.

"We'll get something to graze," said Bernice, "while you talk to Ma."

The curtains were still drawn in the small, musty room, the bed unmade, clothes in a pile on the dressing table at the far end, more tossed on the floor. It was dark and airless and, looking at the bed, Calvin could picture again, as if it were yesterday, Kevin looming over his mother, his hand around her throat.

He closed his eyes to clear the image.

"You still grafting nights, Ma?"

"Nah, got laid off. If it's not the wit ouens taking advantage of us then it's the fuckin' Blacks," she said.

"How did you find me?"

"Y'all think I'm too stupid to see what's going on around me. My boy, I see everything, I just don't say nothin'," she took a cigarette from the pocket of her gown, put it in one corner of her mouth and lit it, her eyes screwing up as she inhaled deeply. "I was pretty sure where ya was going that day, then Uncle Arnold confirmed it," her voice raspy as she held the smoke in. "He was talking to Brian Naidoo's boy. He said he'd seen you at the Club and you tuned him where you was grafting." The smoke snaked out slowly through her mouth and her nostrils. Calvin opened his mouth to say something but Gwennie raised her hand impatiently. "I don't wanna know boy, I don't care. Save your breath. Wat I needs to know is, are you making good sheets?"

"Ya, it's OK. They let me stay for free, they're good to me."

"We need sheets, boy, we got nothin'. That useless, good-for-nothin' Kevin left us without a penny, just like your fuckin' o' man," she was holding the cigarette almost delicately between her gnarled, yellowed fingers, waving it around as she spoke. "Now with this business with Talia, sometimes dunno wat I gone and done to deserve all this shit. Someone up there gotta hate me pretty bad." She stabbed the air with the cigarette and the smoke unfurled towards the ceiling.

"Wat business with Talia? What's going on?"

"She's dropped outta school, says she hates it, doesn't fit in, got no friends. Now she's hooked up with some loser, some druggie. When I try to tell her she can do betta she tunes no other guy's ever gonna want her."

"But she's beautiful."

Gwennie just stared at him, one arm folded across her waist, the other resting on it, holding the cigarette up high.

"Well she is." His voice was a strangled murmur.

"That girl's goin' nowhere fast. Some fuckin' loser comes along and sweet talks her and she thinks he's some kinda hot catch just coz he's the first prick who's ever shown any interest in her. She's gonna get knocked up any minute then I'll have another mouth to feed."

"Talia? No Ma, no way!"

"Wat d'ya know? Ya know your sister? Last time you saw her was four years ago."

"That's not my fault, Ma," he said, his voice low.

"It is wat it is. Last time you saw her she was playing with dolls, now she's sneaking condoms from my dresser."

Calvin felt an overwhelming sadness wash over him, a burden bigger than his young shoulders could bear.

And that was when he made the decision. He had to get Talia help, give her a chance to live her life without the shadow of the scar over her.

By the end of the weekend Calvin had made a deal with her: if she went back to school and broke up with Leroy, he would work extra hard and save money to take her to a doctor and pay for a skin graft to remove her scar.

Initially Talia had acted like it wasn't about the scar, that she just hated school. But she finally broke down and admitted how much she hated herself, hated her looks, her scar.

"You're beautiful as you are Tal, but if ya need for the scar to be gone before ya believe that, I'm gonna do it for ya."

Before he left Calvin gave his mother all the money he had on him, promising to come back in a few weeks' time with more; then he walked the 10km back to the Calderwoods.

CHAPTER
TWENTY-SEVEN

"I LEARNT ALL this from Dr Hodges and, later, from Talia who visits from time-to-time. A lovely, lovely girl," Elizabeth told Emma.

"So what happened with the skin graft?"

"Calvin did as he promised, he literally worked night and day to raise the money and, my dear, I very much doubt it was all legal," said Elizabeth shaking her head sadly. "But for him the means justified the end. The only problem was it left him so exhausted, so physically and mentally drained, that his whole system started to break down. Luckily, by the time he got to that stage, he'd raised just about all the money he needed for Talia."

"Where is she now? How did it all end?"

"The skin graft was successful and the scar was almost entirely removed. The tragedy was that by the time she lay on the operating table to undergo the procedure, unbeknown to anyone, even herself, she was six weeks pregnant with Leroy's child. Calvin worked himself half to death to save her from a life she was already trapped in."

At dinner that evening, Emma kept finding herself glancing at Calvin, unable to reconcile who he was with who he tried so hard to appear to be. Elizabeth's story had left her feeling sad and overwhelmed.

She'd spent most of her life thinking she was the one with the raw deal, wishing for the carefree childhood she saw her friends living; the family bonds which sometimes secured and sometimes constrained but which, at least, were more than this disassociated sensation she felt growing up, apron strings she had never had a chance to outgrow, ripped off too soon.

How different would all their lives have been if that November afternoon, bright blue to disguise the tragedy that awaited them all, could be wiped away. Would Calvin have been left to baby-sit his little sister, just a child himself? Would Peter have died to her? Would she have married Daniel, lusted after Alan? Would Talia be shackled by adult responsibilities before her time? Or Bernice married twice, both disastrously, trying in her mind to cut out a happy family with absolutely no pattern to follow?

Would they have all been so broken?

Elizabeth's voice cut into her day-dreams.

"Emma dear, you seem miles away."

"Oh, sorry about that, I guess I am. I'm thinking I should be getting ready to head home," she said. "I only meant to stay a couple of days, I've already taken advantage of your amazing hospitality."

"Dear, don't think you have to hurry back because of me! It's been wonderful having you, hasn't it Calvin?" she paused while he grunted a vague response. "It can get a little dull just the two of us, especially for Calvin, stuck with a talkative old woman like me. You're welcome to stay just as long as you like."

"Thank you Elizabeth, I really appreciate all you've done," she said, touching the old woman lightly on the arm. "But I'm just putting things off, there's a lot I have to sort out and I can't avoid it forever. I need to look for a job, start earning some money! Besides, Daniel will be wondering if I'm ever coming back." Her attempt at a casual laugh failed dismally, sounding sad and empty instead.

Elizabeth looked at her kindly.

"Stay another week, go on do! Call Daniel and tell him. He'll understand. You've been gone 30 years, I'm sure he can give you one more week. There's so much to try and come to terms with. Tell him, dear," she rested her hand reassuringly on Emma's arm and she nodded.

"Thank you, you've been so kind," was all she could manage.

Calvin was leaning back in his chair watching them and, although his face was swathed in shadows, she thought she saw him smile.

CHAPTER
TWENTY-EIGHT

THE NEXT DAY Emma and Calvin were invited to Clayton's house for Sunday lunch and although he had explicitly invited Elizabeth to join them she declined, saying she was feeling tired and would stay home and rest.

"Are you sure you're OK? I don't have to go, I'd be happy to stay and keep you company," said Emma, a little concerned by the old woman's pallor.

"Nonsense, dear! I'm 78, if I didn't get a little tired now and again I wouldn't be normal," said Elizabeth, sitting at the kitchen table and cupping her hands around a mug of tea. "You go along and have a good time, I have a feeling you're in for a real treat. My goodness, but can those Coloured ladies cook! Mmmmm, my mouth is watering just thinking about it."

They promised to bring her "padkos", or leftovers, and she saw them off, waving goodbye from the shade of the porch.

As they drove off Emma watched in her rear view mirror as the old woman shuffled slowly back into the house and a sense of anxiety settled in her chest.

They headed in the direction of the Club and she marvelled how different everything looked in the daylight.

The houses in Somerset had originally been built as staff accommodation for railway workers. They were all small and square, built close together and enclosed by ramshackle fences. The roofs were corrugated iron, the yards cramped and dusty.

Children played in twos and threes on the side of the streets, riding rusty bicycles, kicking home-made footballs. Gangly teenagers strolled in groups, jeans worn low, baseball caps on back-to-front. They were smoking and laughing. A plump old woman, curlers in her hair, leaned over her gate and shouted at a group of teenagers as they passed. They just laughed and walked on.

They passed a church and saw the congregation spilling out onto the front steps dressed in their Sunday best, the older women wearing bright, broad-brimmed hats. She could imagine Clayton amongst them, dapper in a pin-striped suit and red silk tie.

As it turned out Clayton had attended an earlier service in order to be home in time to welcome them. "They hold three services a day," he said with pride. He had changed into his casual clothes – shorts, a t-shirt and flip flops – looking so different from Friday night Emma almost didn't recognise him.

He was standing in the yard waiting for them to arrive.

"Welcome, welcome!" he said, waving one hand over his head before opening the gate. "Welcome to my humble abode."

Humble it may have been but, on the inside, so spotless you could almost see your reflection in the glare of the polished wooden floors. As Emma stepped over the threshold of the tiny front porch and entered the lounge, small and cluttered with furniture, the smell of delicately-blended spices hit her.

"God that smells amazing," she said and just then a short, squat woman came out of the kitchen, holding a red checked dish towel in her hands and smiling broadly.

"My wife, Ruby," Clayton introduced her with a sweeping gesture of his arm and Emma took a step forward and shook her hand.

"A pleasure to meet you Ruby, thank you so much for having us."

Ruby laughed self-consciously and, despite her age, managed a youthful blush.

"What's your name again, my girl? You'll have to forgive me, my hearing's shot."

Emma leaned in and repeated her name louder in the old woman's ear.

She was amazed that this was Harry's sister, this small, plump old woman, nothing at all like her brother, as Emma remembered him anyway. Although, she noticed, she had his striking green eyes and smooth complexion. And she found herself irrationally thinking how Harry would have looked all these years on.

When Ruby saw her nephew she engulfed him in a bear hug and pulled him down to plant a noisy kiss on his cheek.

"Where you been, boy? You never come see your old Aunt Ruby anymore. What's wrong with you?" And she playfully smacked him across the head as a reprimand.

"Sorry Aunt Rube, always grafting," he said, raising his arms to shield his head.

"Grafting? Huh, that's not what I heard. I heard from Sheila Garnie that you've been seeing Doris Babbage's youngest, that's where you've been spending all your time!" she said, pointing a chubby finger at him.

"Aw Aunt Rube, don't believe everything menses tune ya."

"Yes, don't Rube, your information is unreliable," said Clayton, placing his hand on Calvin's shoulder. "Doris Babbage's youngest isn't the only pretty girl in Somerset he's been seeing. How many lighties you got now Calvin?"

"No lighties, Uncle Clay, no way! I'm smarter than that, no chick's gonna trap me with a lightie."

"Never say never, Calvin, like I'm always telling you, watch yourself." And Clayton was suddenly serious.

Emma watched the exchange and smiled. Is this how it would have been if Harry was still around?

Clayton, noticing her grow thoughtful, gently took her by the arm and led her onto the back porch, motioned for her to take a seat and asked what she'd like to drink.

"Lunch is about half an hour away, what will you have in the meantime? I have beer, vodka, gin, even have some fairly good red wine."

Emma settled for wine and watched Clayton go to a glass-enclosed dresser where all their best China and glassware was displayed and pull out one of their finest wine glasses.

He brought the wine out for her, a can of beer for Calvin, and they sat in the warm sunshine looking out at the little yard.

Ruby had done her best to keep something of a garden going despite the lack of rain, and there was evidence in tiny patchwork flower beds planted with petunias and daisies and a row of hanging baskets trailing long, green creepers.

There was a small chicken run in one corner, two or three dusty hens scratching in it, and an attempt at a vegetable garden in the other. Emma could see rows of lettuce and spinach, as well as vine-shaped tomato plants laden with ripening fruit.

When Clayton saw her looking he got to his feet and offered to show her Ruby's herb garden.

"She carries buckets of water from the bath all the way across here to water her plants. I tell her I'm sure she loves them more than she loves me!" he said with a laugh.

Calvin stayed on the porch, dozing in the sunshine, his beer at his side, while Emma and Clayton wandered off.

He took her to a row of crudely-made herb beds, 10 gallon tin drums which had been cut down the middle, and pointed out her thriving bushes of oregano and thyme, spindly-stalked rosemary and sweet-smelling basil and coriander.

As she bent down to snip off a rosemary leaf and smell it, Clayton knelt down beside her and said in a low voice: "Did you really think I wouldn't know who you are?"

Startled, she turned to look at him. He was looking down at the ground and then continued, "You're the spitting image of her, it'd take a fool not to see that."

"You knew my mother?" Emma was struggling to speak.

"Yes, I knew her. Never met her, yet knew her as well as any of my dearest friends. How could I not when she was all he ever talked about?"

"If you never met her, how did you know how she looked?"

"I'd seen a number of photographs of her, some in the newspaper, others…" and he trailed off abruptly as he saw Ruby come walking over to them.

Emma realised through a look from Clayton that the conversation was between them alone and, as anxious as she was to hear more, she went along with him as he deftly changed the subject.

"My dear lady, I've just been showing Emma your wonderful herb garden," said Clayton, straightening his long, thin legs and standing up.

"It's great, Ruby, I can't tell you how many times I've tried to start a herb garden and failed every time."

"It's the soil, dear," said Ruby in her soft drawl, "African soil, nothing like it in the world. Come live here and you'll be able to grow whatever herbs your heart desires."

"I don't think it's that easy, Ruby."

"Oh, but it is, my dear, everything grows better in our soil – kindness, happiness, love."

"Will you listen to her, my wife the romantic!" said Clayton, wrapping an arm around her shoulders. She was so much smaller than him she fitted snugly under his armpit, straining her head to peer up at him.

Emma smiled to see the two of them and once again was reminded how the formula for happiness had always eluded her.

"How did you two meet?" she asked.

"Harry introduced us," said Clayton. "Minute I met her I knew she was the girl for me."

He smiled down at her and she grinned with pleasure. "Of course I had no idea then I'd be marrying the best Cape Malay cook in the country!"

"You're from Cape Town?" asked Emma.

And replying for her Clayton said, "Her family was. It's a long story. Complicated too. Perhaps some other time. For now I think my dear Ruby has come to call us into the house. Lunch is served."

Lunch was every bit as delicious as Elizabeth had predicted. Ruby had outdone herself, making no less than two curries, one lamb and one chicken, a biryani or mixed rice, home-made rotis – flat bread rolled perfectly round and paper thin before being rapidly fried on a special heavy bottomed plate – fluffy white rice and three types of salad.

For dessert there was trifle and fresh cream and, as if that wasn't enough, one hour after the lunch plates had been cleared away, a double layered chocolate cake served with tea.

Emma plopped back down into the chair on the porch, so full she could hardly move.

"Well there goes about three years' worth of dieting."

"Dieting? Who needs dieting? Us men like a little bit of fat on our women," and he playfully patted Ruby's ample bottom as she passed, laughing as she shrieked with mock offense and swatted his hand away.

After that, content and happy, they all sat in silence. Ruby even dozed off for a while, snoring softly, her head hanging down on her chest. It was almost four o'clock and the sun's intensity was beginning to wane. Sunlight filtered down through the massive flamboyant trees in the back yard, casting lace shadows over the porch.

"I had no idea it was so late; we should be heading home," Emma said looking over at Calvin who stood up languidly and stretched.

"Ya, thanks Auntie, Uncle, I scheme we'd better jol, the o' queen will be waiting for us."

When Emma put out her hand to shake Clayton's he took it, then pulled her gently to him and wrapped her in a bear hug.

"Emma, Emma my dear, you worry too much, don't fret so, everything will be fine," he said with warmth, and she smiled into his shoulder, not sure she believed it. Then, just as she was pulling away, he took her hand and discreetly pressed an envelope into it. "Wait till you get home," he said with a wink. She quickly slipped it into her handbag.

They were both quietly reflective on the way home, lulled by the good food and the tranquillity of the afternoon. Emma realised with a guilty stab that she'd enjoyed herself so much she'd hardly thought about Elizabeth all afternoon and now the nagging anxiety returned and she found herself speeding up to get to the house faster.

"Wat's the rush?"

"Nothing, just want to get back to Elizabeth. She wasn't looking so well this morning."

He grunted and sat upright.

When they arrived at the house all was silent and Emma walked tentatively over to Elizabeth's door and knocked gently. There was no reply and she knocked a little louder. Still no sound from within so she turned the handle and went in, walking over to the old woman's bed and gently calling her name.

It took Emma about five seconds to realise there was something wrong, and another five to breathlessly run out the door, screaming for Calvin.

Hearing the panic in her voice he bolted out of the apartment, hurriedly shrugging on a shirt. "Wat? Wat's cutting?"

"Elizabeth! It's Elizabeth!" She'd hardly blurted out the words and he was tearing into the house and into the old woman's room.

Emma was right behind him. "We need to call an ambulance," she said, trying her best to stay calm.

"No!" And he was already sliding an arm under her shoulders, another under her frail legs, "They take too long, we have to jol with her."

Emma grabbed the car keys and a bed spread and ran outside. Calvin was already at the car, holding Elizabeth to his chest with one hand while opening the back door with his other. He lay her on the back seat and Emma handed him the cover which he spread over the old woman.

Then they jumped into the front seat and sped away, Calvin shouting out directions to the hospital, glancing continually at the back seat at the old woman's deathly white pallor and her utter stillness.

They drove around to the emergency ward and, somewhere in the haze, Emma registered it was the hospital where she and Peter had been born.

She had barely cut off the engine before Calvin was leaping out of the car and opening the back door. She raced in to get help, but, by the time she returned with a male nurse and a stretcher, Calvin was already running up the steps, cradling Elizabeth in his arms.

The nurse helped him lay her on the stretcher and she was rolled away down the corridor, leaving Emma and Calvin staring after her.

The receptionist was patient but firm. They were to fill in the forms and then take a seat in the waiting room until the doctor came out. No-one was allowed to accompany her into the ward, especially since neither of them was family.

"We need to contact her kids," said Emma and, nodding, Calvin walked outside to make the call. And then there was nothing to do but wait.

They sat on opposite ends of the small room, each deep in their own thoughts.

After about an hour of sitting in silence, Emma walked over to the reception desk but there was still no word from the doctor.

She was feeling claustrophobic and walked outside into the small enclosed courtyard to get some fresh air. She leaned against the cool, brick wall, tilted back her head and closed her eyes. She had never felt so tired.

It was then that she remembered the envelope Clayton had handed her and rummaged inside her handbag until she found it. She pulled it out and slid her finger under the flap, reached inside and pulled out a small, square photograph.

It was old and faded and quite difficult to see in the dim light, so Emma walked back inside and looked at it under the fluorescent light.

The two figures caught in the image were unmistakable: she was sitting on the bonnet of an old car, he was standing next to her, his arm around her waist. They were looking directly into the camera and smiling, their faces radiant.

She turned it over and, on the back, in her mother's sloping, looping hand-writing, were the words: *To Harry. Forever yours. M.*

CHAPTER
TWENTY-NINE

Emma 1976

EMMA'S FATHER WAS expecting his conscription papers long before they arrived. Every able-bodied White man between the ages of 18 and 55 was being called up to fight in the war. Her father was 35 years old.

The war was all anyone seemed to talk about at school: whose father had been called up, who'd been killed in action, how many 'terrs' Butch Walker's father had single-handedly killed in contact.

It scared Emma and she didn't want to think about it but it was everywhere she looked, even across the breakfast table on the front pages of the newspaper her father would pore over each morning.

One morning the front page had featured, in gruesome detail, a photograph of a mutilated villager, tortured at the hands of "terrorists". Emma had run to the bathroom and vomited, then cried all the way to school.

Her father was unsympathetic, insisting she pull herself together and learn to toughen up.

"These are the facts, Emma, this is what these kaffirs do to their own people. Best you find out sooner rather than later what kind of animals we're dealing with."

When she came home from school her mother took her in her arms and hugged her tightly.

"How are you feeling, honey?" she asked, holding Emma close to her and stroking her hair.

"I'm scared Mama."

"Scared of what, sweetheart?"

"Scared of the terror-orists."

"There are no terrorists in town, my love, we're safe here, the troops are protecting us."

"But Daddy says they hate White people."

"It's a lot more complicated than that, honey."

"How complicated?"

"You're too young to understand now, but maybe one day."

Peter was a little more informative.

"The Blacks say this is their country and the Whites took it without asking and they want it back and they don't mind dying to get it," he said all in one long breath.

"But if they're dead, what good is it?" she asked wide-eyed.

"No good to them, but maybe to their kids, or their kids' kids."

"What 'bout us?"

"What about us?"

"What's gonna happen to us?"

"Who knows? If we win – which Dad says we will – we'll be fine. If not, we have to leave."

"Leave? Leave to where? I don't want to go nowhere!"

"No-one's going anywhere right now silly billy," he said, shoving her lightly on the arm. "Come on, let's go up to the fort."

And the dark clouds of the war and the confusing politics of grown-ups were momentarily forgotten under the dappled green leaves of the mulberry tree.

CHAPTER THIRTY

THE FIRST TIME Emma's father walked out of the bedroom wearing his army uniform his chest was puffed out, his chin held high.

While Peter clapped and Emma shrieked with delight, seeing him in his camouflage and brown army boots laced up his calf, Margot busied herself at the sink, her back to them.

"So honey, what do you think?" he called into the kitchen.

"Very nice." Not even looking up from the dishes she was washing in the sink.

"What is it, baby, don't think green's my colour?"

No response. So he marched into the kitchen, came up behind her and wrapped his arms around her, pinning her down.

"Hey honey?" he said, but the playfulness in his voice was gone.

He was squeezing her tight and pressing his cheek against the side of her head. Margot was squirming, but he wasn't letting go.

"What is it my communist beauty? Worried I'm gonna kill all the terrorist scum? Your precious Black brethren? I'm damn well gonna try my best." And just as suddenly as he'd taken her into his arms he released her and walked away.

The next day, up in the tree, Emma asked Peter about it.

"Why doesn't Mama like Daddy's uniform?"

"It's not the uniform."

"What is it then?"

"Dunno."

"Why did Daddy get cross when Mama didn't like it?"

"Dunno."

"But Daddy was so mad."

"Maybe he likes the war and Mama doesn't."

"Why doesn't Mama like it?"

"Dunno. You ask too many questions. Why don't you ask Mama yourself?"

In the evening when her mother lay down beside her as she did for a few minutes every night before putting her to bed, Emma asked her why she didn't like the war.

Her mother's blue eyes darkened as she remembered the ugly scene the children had witnessed.

"Oh Emma, honey, it's not as easy as all that. No-one wants to see people they love going off to war, getting killed for nothing."

"But it's not for nothing is it Mama? Daddy says it's to save our homes from the Blacks.

"'Is that what he said, honey? It's hard to say whose home it is, darling. Everyone thinks of it as their home; how do we decide who goes and who stays?"

"Why does anyone have to go, Mama? Why can't everyone just stay?"

"Exactly my love, if only adults could see it that way."

"So you're scared about Daddy getting hurt?"

"Yes, honey, and all the Daddies and brothers and uncles who are going off to war. The Blacks and the Whites."

"The Blacks have Daddies and Mommies and brothers and sisters too, Mama?"

"Yes of course they have families, honey, they're people just like you and me."

"Daddy says they're animals."

"And they probably think we are. It's so hard to understand, sweetheart, and I can't promise it will get any easier as you get older. Somewhere along the way humans decided they had to be recognised by things that don't really matter at all – the colour of their skin, the language they speak, the way they dress. Now we're all just caught in the middle of that mess and we don't know how to get out."

"So we have wars?"

"Yes, honey, you could say that. So we have wars. Making us hate each other even more."

"I don't hate Blacks, Mama."

"I know you don't, sweetheart, because you're wise and kind and sensible."

"And you don't hate them Mama."

"No, honey, I don't."

"And what's a communist, Mama?"

Margot took a sharp breath. "Right, sweetheart, I think that's enough questions for one night. It's late and you need to get to sleep. We'll talk another time."

"Ok Mama."

"Good night honey," she said kissing her daughter gently on the forehead.

"Good night Mama."

Her mother rose from the bed, stroked her cheek and started walking towards the door.

As she reached it and lifted her hand to turn off the light, Emma called out softly, her voice bleary with sleep. "Mama, I'm gonna be a communist when I grow up."

A shadow of a smile passed across Margot's face. "I'd keep that to myself if I were you my darling. I love you." And she switched off the light.

CHAPTER
THIRTY-ONE

HARRY STARTED STAYING on the property when Emma's father was called up on active duty.

"Harry, my boy," said David one evening as he pulled in at the gate, and Margot flinched.

"Harry my boy, come over here, I need to talk to you."

The two men walked off together to the porch, Harry walking a few steps behind him.

"I wonder if you can do something for me, I wonder if you can spend a few nights a week on the property, you know, keeping an eye on the family for me? I'll pay you handsomely my boy, you know I've always taken care of you."

There was nowhere Harry would rather be.

It was agreed he would spend Monday to Friday at the house, sleeping in the servants' quarters at the back, and going home on weekends to be with his family.

Before long he was also spending the odd weekend at the Hardy's and, by the time David was on his third call-up duty, Harry was practically a permanent resident.

When David came home on leave, Harry would be dispatched home but Emma couldn't help but notice he never looked very happy to go.

She once asked her mother about it.

"Mama, doesn't Harry like his family?"

"Like his family? Why, of course he does, sweetheart, he loves them. What would make you say a thing like that?"

"He looks sad when he goes." And Emma watched startled surprise and then sadness pass over her mother's face. "Maybe he misses you," said Emma.

"Misses us," said her mother quickly, "he probably gets used to being here, playing with you and Peter, and misses you when he goes. Now come on, let's go see what Peter's up to." She changed the subject abruptly and walked away, Emma running after her to look for Peter.

One of the last times Harry came to stay he had exciting news. He arrived on his bicycle as usual, but told the children he'd bought a car.

"Next time I come I'll be driving my own car," he said.

They couldn't wait to see it and persuaded their mother to drive them to Harry's friend's house where it was parked.

It was a baby blue VW Beetle, a 1964 model with large round headlights that reminded Emma of a big smiling face.

She laughed with delight and skipped over to where it was parked under a sprawling fire-red flamboyant tree.

"Needs a lot of work," said Harry, the pride in his voice unmistakeable, "but I think I can get her going in time for Christmas."

He glanced over at Margot and when she smiled her approval he beamed.

The children soon got bored with looking at the car and took off towards the back of the house to play with a tyre that had been standing up against the wall. As they were rolling it around the corner Emma glanced back and saw her mother hand Harry's friend a camera. He took it from her then motioned for them to pose on the bonnet. And Emma watched as Harry slipped his arm around her mother's waist and they both smiled into the lens.

CHAPTER
THIRTY-TWO

EMMA WAS STILL staring at the photograph when she heard Calvin calling her. She quickly tucked it back into her handbag.

"Come, they're calling us, the o' queen's awake!"

She ran after him down the corridor and to the reception desk where the nurse directed them to Elizabeth's ward.

There was a doctor bending over her and, when they paused in the open doorway, he looked up and motioned for them to come in.

Elizabeth's eyes were half-open slits in her small, sunken face.

"She needs to rest so I'm only going to allow five minutes with her," said the doctor, "I'll meet you outside afterwards."

Emma allowed Calvin to go in front but when she sensed his deep apprehension she quickened her pace and came up alongside him.

At the head of the bed she looked down at the old woman and took her cold hand. "Oh Elizabeth, you gave us the fright of our lives, how are you feeling?"

Her lips were pale and parched and she moved them slightly but no words came out.

She carried on holding her hand, stroking it gently.

Calvin stood slightly to one side, shifting uncomfortably from one foot to the other, hands clasped behind his back. Emma had never seen him look so vulnerable.

They stayed a few moments longer, Emma still holding the old woman's hand, Calvin still staring on uncertainly. Their five minutes up, Emma leaned close to Elizabeth's ear, whispered good night, and the two of them left the ward.

The doctor was up the hall, seeing to another patient. When he finally emerged he led them to his consulting room and motioned for them to take a seat.

They sat in silence for the first few moments, the doctor staring intently at the chart in front of him. Calvin and Emma waited anxiously for him to speak.

He cleared his throat, put the chart down on the desk in front of him and began. "I don't think I need to tell you that Mrs Calderwood is a very sick woman. I should be telling this to her next of kin, but I believe they're not here and, by the time they come, it could be too late."

"Too late?" Emma's voice was strangled breath.

"Mrs Calderwood has suffered a stroke which has rendered her almost entirely incapacitated. The real danger, the very present fear, is that she could have a second. She's weak and frail and her metabolism will definitely not sustain another attack. We're doing all we can but she's not a young woman. If it wasn't for the machines, we would have already lost her."

Emma didn't dare look at Calvin.

"What do you suggest, doctor?" she asked.

"I suggest her children get here as soon as possible and that we pray very, very hard." He was gentle but matter-of-fact, having delivered bad news too many times to allow himself the luxury of sentimentality.

"We'll be moving her from the emergency ward to the ICU where she'll have the high care medical attention she needs. You'll be able to see her there during visiting hours." And he closed the chart, indicating that the interview was over. "If you'll forgive me, we have a car accident victim arriving by ambulance any minute. I must be there when he arrives."

Emma stood up shakily, thanked the doctor and the two of them left. It was only when they walked out of the hospital and saw the auburn smudge of light glowing on the horizon that they realised it was almost morning.

The sun rose as they drove, in silence, back to the house, spreading its warm glow like creamy butter over the dawn sky.

CHAPTER
THIRTY-THREE

ELIZABETH'S BOYS FLEW in on the lunch time flight from Johannesburg the following day. They arrived at the hospital exactly 35 minutes after she died.

Calvin and Emma had spent the morning visiting hours sitting at her side, trying not to look at the tubes and machines reaching like tentacles into her, coaxing out her last breath.

The nurses said she hadn't regained consciousness since arriving in ICU in the early hours of the morning.

They were on their way to pick up Elizabeth's sons from the airport when the call came, but Calvin's phone had been on silent from the visit to ICU earlier and it hadn't rung, so the first they heard of her death was when the four of them arrived at the hospital to see her just after 2p.m.

By then her bed had already been stripped and the machines cleared away, ready for the next admission.

Emma had never felt more of an intruder, standing by the narrow empty bed, still warm with Elizabeth's body, with her three sons. Steve and Jack were crying openly, Calvin stood as still as stone, his square jaw set, his face dark and brooding.

She quietly turned and left, leaving them to mourn their mother in private, and walked downstairs to the hospital parking lot. She sat on a bench across from the tiny caravan where visitors could buy last-minute gifts of half-wilted roses and melted chocolates for their loves ones and sobbed like her heart would break: for Elizabeth, for her sons, for Calvin, for herself and all the lost dreams.

She must have sat there for over an hour, oblivious to the people streaming past her towards the hospital doors, staring at her as she sat there, quietly crying.

Finally she stood, her tears all dried up, feeling as wrung out as a squeezed sponge, and walked back into the hospital. She found Steve and Jack sitting with the hospital administrator going over paperwork, but Calvin was nowhere in sight.

She waited down the hall for them. When they finished they walked up to her in the corridor.

"I am so, so sorry for your loss," said Emma, walking towards them. "I'd only just met your mother but felt like I'd known her all my life. What an amazing woman she was, I feel so privileged to have met her," and she could feel the tears welling up in her eyes again.

"Thank you, Emma," said Steve.

She had briefly explained in the car on the way from the airport who she was and how she happened to be living in their mother's house, but still felt awkward to be there at a time like this.

Walking back to the parking lot towards her car, she asked where Calvin was but no-one had seen him.

"He must have slipped away while we were in ICU. I haven't seen him since," said Jack.

They looked around for him but finally concluded he was no longer at the hospital and had probably found his own way home.

"I want to help in any way I can," said Emma on the drive back to the house, "I'm completely at your disposal for transport or any help you may need with funeral arrangements. But I think it best I move back to the hotel and leave you to yourselves, you need your privacy at a time like this."

"Our mother invited you to stay at the house and we're happy to have you, it's no problem at all," said Steve.

But Emma insisted and, when they reached the house, went straight to her room and started packing her bags.

Calvin was not at the house. He wasn't there later in the afternoon when Emma cooked a quick pasta dish and the three of them sat on the porch to eat an early dinner. Neither was he there when, after dinner, she packed her bags into the car, said good-bye to Steve and Jack, and returned to the Holiday Inn.

Once she'd checked into her hotel room she tried calling him on his cell but there was no reply. Drained and exhausted, she collapsed on top of the bed covers around nine, intending to shower and get under the sheets after a quick nap, but fell into a deep sleep and only woke at dawn.

After breakfast she went around to the house to see if there was anything she could do to help and was surprised to hear that Calvin had still not shown up.

"Are there times when he doesn't spend the night at home?" asked Jack.

"Not since I've been here. But I haven't been here long, maybe he's staying with a friend."

There was a lot to do in preparation for the funeral, set for two days' time, and Emma offered to go along as moral support. They spent a hectic morning running between the hospital, the funeral parlour and the government offices to try and obtain a death certificate. After returning twice and being told three different stories, they finally succumbed to paying a bribe and had the certificate within 15 minutes.

"Good old Zimbabwe," said Steve, "there are some things you can always rely on."

After organising the church and the flowers, they went back to the house. There was still no sign of Calvin and, her anxiety mounting, Emma headed back to the hotel.

She was somehow relieved to leave the house, crowded as it was with ghosts which, up until then had been diffused by Elizabeth's kindly, tranquil presence.

Back in the impersonal hotel room she tried to rest easy and assimilate her thoughts, but it wasn't working. She was restless and anxious and couldn't settle down. Eventually she placed a call to Daniel to tell him about the old woman's death and explain that she'd be staying a little longer to help the family wind down her affairs. Once again there was no answer on the land line and she couldn't face another awkward cell phone conversation like the last. So instead she went down to the internet café and sent him a brief e-mail.

Dear Daniel,

I hope you're well. Old Mrs Calderwood, the woman who bought the house from my parents and with whom I've been staying, had a stroke day before yesterday and died. It's been a great shock to everyone. Her sons have come up from South Africa but I've offered to stay on and help with arrangements; they have no family left here and all Elizabeth's friends are too old to be able to offer much assistance. Looks like I'll be here for another week or so, just thought I'd let you know.

Then she hesitated before adding: *I tried calling the house to explain everything to you, thought you'd be home since it was 11pm your time, but there was no reply.* She pressed "send" before she could change her mind.

As she was typing she noticed the green light come on next to Alan's name, indicating that he was on line. She ignored it and quickly signed out.

CHAPTER
THIRTY-FOUR

IN THE EVENING Emma called the house to see if Calvin had resurfaced, but no-one had seen or heard from him. His cell phone was now on voice mail.

She decided she couldn't sit around any longer doing nothing.

Grabbing a jacket and her handbag she ran out of the hotel room and down the elevator to the car park. She had no idea where he was or where to start looking. The first place she could think of was the sports bar in town.

It was a Tuesday night, but the parking spaces outside the bar were all taken. She drove up and down both sides of the road before she finally saw a pair of reverse lights go on and pulled into a parking space.

She recognised the bouncer at the door and asked if he'd seen Calvin. When he looked blank she quickly remembered. "Crab, Crab, have you seen Crab?" shouting over the music and the laughter spilling out from the bar onto the pavement outside.

He shrugged and shook his huge head then turned his attention back to the flood of people trying to get in at the door.

Next she tried the pub overlooking the lake, but still nothing. As she was getting into her car she saw a lanky form with a looping walk slink behind a pillar by the car park. She was sure it was Calvin's cousin, Elroy, and wandered tentatively towards the shadows and called out his name.

Elroy jumped out from behind the pillar, suspicion and guilt written all over his face. A stocky man standing with him was stuffing a packet into his pocket.

When he saw her standing there he instantly relaxed and hollered over to the man: "It's cool, it's cool, it's my cuzzie's chick." Then, leering at her, added "Hey sweet thing, you come to get some of what Elroy's got?"

"No Elroy, I'm not. I'm looking for Calvin, have you seen him?"

"No baby, I ain't seen 'im, but I'm here."

"Right now I need to find Calvin, it's urgent. Do you have any idea where he could be?"

"Baby," he drawled, "do I look like his fuckin' keeper? I don't think so. But if you change ya mind just ask for Elroy, I'll be waitin' for ya."

She didn't bother to reply and headed back to her car.

She sat with her hands on the steering wheel thinking for a few minutes, wondering where to try next. And then she thought of Clayton.

"Of course!" she said out-loud and, as she drove off, spotted Elroy swaggering back into the shadows, hand-in-hand with a girl no older than 14, halter-neck dress pulled tight across her flat chest and boyish hips.

Emma thought again about Calvin and a tight fearful knot formed in the pit of her stomach.

CHAPTER
THIRTY-FIVE

DRIVING THROUGH THE darkened streets of Somerset Emma realised that she didn't know the way as well as she'd imagined; every street, every house looked exactly the same. When she inadvertently drove in a complete loop and ended up where she had started, she decided to ask for help.

She pulled into a garage and asked for directions to the Club, knowing that once she found that, she'd easily recognise Clayton's house.

Less than five minutes later she was passing the mosque and pulling up at Clayton's gate. The house was in complete darkness and she hesitated, but her anxiety for Calvin was growing and she knew Clayton would understand. She pressed the car horn and waited.

There was no response. She hooted again and this time a light came on in one of the front rooms and a sliver of fluorescence shone onto the porch as a curtain was pulled back.

She saw the window open and a man's voice call out: "Who's there?"

"It's Emma, Clayton," she said, stepping out of the car. "I'm so sorry to disturb you, but it's urgent."

"Emma? What's wrong?" he said, even as she heard the front door unlock and open and saw Clayton step out.

"It's Calvin," she said before he was even half-way down the drive-way. "I don't know if you heard, but Mrs Calderwood died yesterday and Calvin's been missing ever since. I'm getting worried."

"The old lady died? But how?"

"A stroke, it happened while we were here, having lunch with you Sunday." She was standing with one foot on the ground, the other still in the cab, her hand resting on the open car door. "There was probably nothing anyone could have done, even if we'd been home. She made it to the hospital but died yesterday. Calvin was completely broken up. He was at the hospital one minute, gone the next. You know Calvin…"

"Yes, my dear, I know Calvin alright," said Clayton. "Give me a minute, I'll just get dressed then come with you."

Clayton was still shrugging on his shirt when he walked out the door, turning to lock it and then racing down the drive-way towards her.

"Ok, my dear, we have a couple of options," he said before he'd even sat down in the passenger seat and closed the car door.

CHAPTER
THIRTY-SIX

EMMA FOLLOWED CLAYTON'S directions to Gwennie's house, the first place he could think of trying, and they eventually pulled up outside a derelict apartment block, facing out onto a dusty courtyard. A rusted body of a car hulked to one side, its doors, scraped clean of paint, wide open, making it look in the dark like some grotesque insect about to lumber off into the sky.

The lights were on in three or four of the square windows and Clayton grunted with satisfaction to see that number 12, on the second floor, was one of them.

"They're awake," he said under his breath, though he sounded anything but relieved. "Emma, my dear, I probably don't need to tell you Gwennie isn't the easiest person, just keep your wits about you. If you want to stay in the car I understand, I can go upstairs alone and check."

"No, I'm coming with you," she said.

They walked across the dark courtyard and started up the stairs, so narrow they had to walk in single file.

"You OK?" asked Clayton, glancing back at her.

"I'm fine." She was groping her way up each dark step, feeling for the balustrade, rough and grimy under her hand.

They were half-way up the steps when they heard loud voices and the sound of either a television or radio being played at full volume.

At the second floor landing Clayton paused momentarily for Emma to catch up with him and then carried on along the dark corridor until he reached number 12. He hesitated, but only slightly, before he lifted his hand and knocked.

"Who the fuck is that?"

"Gwennie, it's Clayton. Sorry to trouble you at this late hour, can you please open up?"

"Clayton who?"

He sighed, "Clayton Smith."

"Wat the fuck d'ya want?" And before the sentence was even out she had snatched open the door and was standing in front of them.

"Gwennie," said Clayton, bowing slightly.

She glared at him, her eyes hard, her hair a mess of wild curls framing her small face. She was smaller than Emma expected with traces in her large eyes and full mouth of the good looking woman she must have once been. Today her face was withered and worn, dark smudges under her eyes.

Her skin was parchment dry, stretched so thin and tight over her bones it looked like it may split.

Her faded pink towelling gown was tied loosely at the waist, falling open to reveal her withered neck and thin, sunken chest, the collarbone jutting out sharply through the sallow skin.

"Who the fuck is this?" she said, jutting her chin in Emma's direction.

"A friend," he answered without missing a beat.

Emma nodded but received no response.

"We're looking for Calvin."

"How the fuck would I know where he is?"

"Well Gwennie, you are his mother."

"I fuckin' well know I'm his mother! The question is, do we know who's his father?" And with that she threw back her head and cackled.

"Well, perhaps that's an issue we can debate some other time," said Clayton, cutting her off mid-cackle.

"That's an issue we can debate some other time," she said in a mocking jeer. "Mr high-and-mighty! Mr I'm-too-fucking-good-for-you-Smith. Huh! Why don't ya just admit it, ya no better than the rest of us!"

"Now Gwennie," said Clayton, maintaining his poise, "I didn't come here to pick a fight, just to find out if you know where Calvin is. Old Mrs Calderwood died yesterday and Calvin's gone missing. I thought, even if you didn't know where he was, you'd like to know."

With that she sobered slightly. "The old lady's dead? What about Calvin's graft?"

"It's just happened, Gwennie, no-one knows anything yet. Her sons are here from South Africa, they're sorting things out."

"They better look after my son, he was there looking after their o' queen when they couldn't give a fuck, they better sort him out."

"I'm sure they appreciate all Calvin's done, Gwennie, and will be fair to him. But it's a little too early for all that. For now we just have to focus on finding Calvin, you know how fond of the old woman he was. He's probably taking it badly, grieving for her somewhere. I worry what he may do."

"Ya, worried more about the old bitch than he did about his own mother," she said.

"Now you know that's not true, Gwennie."

"You don't fuckin' tell me what's true and what's not true, do ya hear me?" Her eyes were wild.

"Who is it Mom?" asked a quiet voice. A young woman appeared by her side, half a moon face peering tentatively out. "Oh hello Uncle Clayton," she smiled, her eyes lighting up with recognition."

Before he replied Emma already knew: this was Talia.

"Hello Talia dear."

Talia smiled shyly.

"They're looking for Calvin," Gwennie spat.

"Calvin? Why, what's happened?" Her smile crumpled.

"Nothing my dear, I'm sure he's fine. It's just that the old lady died and he's upset, and he's taken himself off somewhere and we want to find him," said Clayton.

"Elizabeth's dead?" Talia's eyes widened.

"What d'ya fucking know about Elizabeth?" Gwennie said the name mockingly.

"I knew her," Talia shrank from her mother and Emma realised Gwennie had no idea about her visits to the old woman.

"Well, we don't know where he is. When you find him tell him we need sheets," said Gwennie. And with that she declared the interview closed and made to close the door.

Clayton gently but firmly put his hand out and barred the door from closing. Then he looked Gwennie calmly in the eye. "Your son needs you right now, Gwennie. Probably needs you more than he ever has."

Gwennie paused. Then she threw back her head, pursed her lips and spat square in his face.

Both Talia and Emma gasped, but Clayton merely closed his eyes, calmly reached into his pocket for a handkerchief and slowly and methodically wiped his face.

"Thank you, Gwennie, always a pleasure." And he turned to leave.

Emma followed, unable to mask her disdain as she glanced back at Gwennie one last time, standing in the doorway, hand on her hip, and Talia's gentle moon face staring out from behind her.

They had only just reached the car when they heard footsteps and turned around to see Talia running towards them. She carried a child in her arms and was breathless with exertion.

"Wait! Wait up, please!" she called. "I'm coming with you."

As they drew closer, Emma realised the child was about 10 years old, her thin legs dangling almost to the floor as Talia struggled to hold her. Her face was expressionless and, when Talia saw Emma looking searchingly at her, she said: "This is my daughter, Sabrina. Sabrina, say hello, this is Uncle Clayton and…"

"Emma, Emma Groves, I'm a friend of Calvin's."

"And Emma," said Talia. "Say hello."

Sabrina moaned slightly, her head lolling unsteadily on her thin neck.

"Sorry, but I had to bring her along, no-one at home's gonna look after her."

Talia was five months pregnant before anyone suspected. She was only two months pregnant when Leroy hit her for the first time.

It was a hard, open-handed slap across the face, so hard and unexpected that first time, she lost her balance and fell against the kitchen wall. The slap bruised her delicate skin a deep mauve, on the site of her recently removed burn mark. For a whole week afterwards her hated marks were back, and she found herself styling her hair to hide that side of her face again.

The doctor said it probably wasn't that first slap which had caused Sabrina's birth defects. It was more than likely the kick to her belly at seven months, the one that sent her tumbling backwards down the stairs.

Talia lay semi-conscious at the foot of the steps, a pool of blood seeping through her skirt and spreading out onto the ground, forming shiny red droplets which sat like tiny, ripe berries over the dusty surface.

Sabrina was born two months premature, cut from Talia's belly as she writhed and haemorrhaged in the ambulance on the way to the hospital. Paramedics were fighting to save the lives of mother and child, and sliced into her before the anaesthetic had fully kicked in. Talia felt every slice of the scalpel, every desperate grasp of the fingers struggling to pull her baby free.

Afterwards, lying in the hospital ward, she felt torn, inside and out. And when her baby girl was laid in her tired arms, she was in too much pain to lift her up to look at her. All she saw was the smooth curve of her round head, her long dark lashes resting on her high cheekbones.

That was all she needed to fall in love with her.

The first person who came to the hospital to visit Talia was Calvin. His eyes were darkly-shadowed, his jaw set. But when he saw Talia and Sabrina lying there together his face softened.

He took Sabrina in his arms and cradled her, then kissed her lightly on the forehead.

As he handed her back to his baby sister he leaned in close to Talia and kissed her lightly on the cheek.

Then he turned and left.

No-one missed Leroy, a drifter who'd had 12 different homes in 17 years and been in and out of the local home for juvenile delinquents most of his life. No-one mourned him when his body was found in a grassy verge just outside Somerset, his throat slashed.

Talia read about his death in the newspaper the day she asked Calvin to be Sabrina's godfather, the same day doctors told her that her little girl was severely brain-damaged.

Leroy's killer was never found. Police, short of manpower and low on resources, closed the case after two years due to lack of evidence, concluding it was the result of a drunken brawl. Not the first, not the last.

CHAPTER
THIRTY-SEVEN

1977

WHAT HAPPENED BETWEEN Harry and Margot once David was conscripted would be easy to over-simplify: the passionate longing of a wife whose husband was away at war, the close proximity of a hot-blooded attractive man. An accident just waiting to happen.

But there was more to it than that. Harry didn't fall in love with Margot for her looks, even though they almost took his breath away the first time he saw her.

He fell in love with her when he watched her with her children.

Harry didn't mean to stare, but he found himself doing it the whole time. There was something so pure and gentle in the way she looked at her children, the patience with which she bent down to their level, looked deep into their eyes and listened to them, the gentleness with which she'd brush a tear away or bandage a grazed knee. Everything about her exuded love and he was utterly captivated.

Part of the attraction was the deep contrast to Gwennie, a woman he'd married out of duty when she fell pregnant with Calvin, and whom he'd never managed to learn to love unconditionally. Where Margot was soft and maternal, Gwennie was tough and unforgiving; where Margot seemed somehow naïve and other-worldly, Gwennie was hardened and street-wise.

He wanted to protect Margot from the harshness of the world, the evils of the war. He wanted to protect her from her husband.

He winced, almost as if he'd been struck, every time he saw David wield his territorial power over her, grab her roughly, pull her close and demand her attention. It took all his self-restraint to look away and not react.

But Margot was no walk-over and in her own quiet way she defied David more and more, standing her ground and resisting his demands.

With her husband away, Harry and Margot inevitably spent more time together, not only in discussing the chores and duties around the house, normally handled by David, but also finding themselves in discussions about the war, the children, the weather, any mundane topic Harry could dream up to keep her near him.

She enjoyed his company and found herself wandering out into the garden to find him in the quiet mornings when the children were at school, sitting on a step near him and talking to him while he worked.

The first time Harry touched her was lightly with the tips of his fingers, softly tracing a line from her centre parting across her smooth forehead and down the side of her cheek, his hand coming to rest in the sweet, warm place where her neck and shoulder met. When he removed his fingers and placed his lips there instead, he felt her soft skin shudder.

He slowly raised his head from her neck and brushed his lips against hers. Her breath was sweet and hot and as he pressed harder against her soft lips he closed his eyes.

They'd been standing at the back of the house, a few steps away from his room. She'd come out looking for him after dark, once she'd put the children to bed. A light had gone out in the kitchen. It could have been anything, a blown bulb, a faulty switch, a broken water tap. The path she took out to the back of the house that night was an inevitable, pre-ordained track they could no longer avoid. But when she called out to him and he came out of his room towards her, she couldn't find the words to speak. She just stood and stared at him. He took a few steps closer, looked deeply into her eyes, then silently reached out and touched her.

It was only a few short steps to his room and he wanted more than anything else in the world to take her in his arms and carry her to his narrow bed. But he didn't. Not that first night. Instead he gently stopped kissing her and wrapped his arms around her, pressing his body close to hers. And the two of them stood there, anchored by their deep desire, for what felt like an eternity, his breath in her hair, his powerful arms holding her tight.

CHAPTER
THIRTY-EIGHT

AS THEY DROVE, Clayton in the passenger seat directing her, Talia holding Sabrina in the back, Emma felt again the nagging sensation of memory that had gripped her when she'd first met Calvin. And still it evaded her. Something about the dark, narrow streets they were passing through, the feeling of fear and recognition like two hooded villains – good cop, bad cop – haunting her again.

"Emma, are you OK? I said turn left," Clayton's voice startled her out of her tattered reverie.

"Oh Lord, sorry, I missed it."

"It's OK, try a u-turn up ahead, it's clear."

She manoeuvred the car in a wide turn, barely missing a canal which perpetually ran with foul smelling waste from the industrial area, and headed back in the direction Clayton had indicated.

"Emma, maybe it's not a good time to bring this up, but there may not be another opportunity. How much, dear, did you know about Harry, about what happened to him afterwards?"

Emma, startled, glanced across at Clayton's face, the worry lines in his brow accentuated by the lights of a passing car.

211

"After it happened? Nothing, hardly anything at all. My brother and I were sent off to an aunt in the States. I always just presumed…." she left the sentence unfinished.

Clayton glanced nervously back at Talia and watched as the glint of recognition finally dawned in her eyes.

"You said you're a friend of Calvin's?" Talia asked quietly from the back seat.

"Um, yes."

"Where do you know him from?"

"She's Margot Hardy's daughter, Talia."

"What?" gasped Talia.

"I'm sorry," said Emma, unsure what else to say. She looked back at Talia in the rear view mirror and saw her wide-eyed horror.

"I don't believe it."

They drove on in silence, the atmosphere thick with tension. And Emma couldn't shake the unreasonable thought from her head that had fate dealt them all a different hand, had circumstances been different, they might have been friends.

CHAPTER
THIRTY-NINE

1977

ONCE THEY SURRENDERED to the desire, there was no turning back. The first night, after putting the children to bed, Margot locked the house and gingerly picked her way through the garden to Harry's room. She'd lifted her hand to knock on his door but, before she could do so, he'd opened it, as if he'd been waiting for her. The second night he was waiting for her just outside the kitchen door, and from then on, he was there every night.

They would allow themselves no more than two hours together, then Harry would walk her back to the house, kiss her longingly on the kitchen steps, and wait while she went inside and locked the door. What she didn't know was that he often stayed there for a long time afterwards, listening to her footsteps padding through the house, checking that all the doors were locked, the lights turned off, hearing her pause at the doorway to each of the children's rooms and then retreat to her own.

He would imagine her every graceful move, the silky smooth curves of her skin as she undressed, the honey shine of her softly waving hair, her long, slender limbs stretching out under the cool cotton.

Then he would slowly make his way back to his room and sleep with his face buried in sheets still fresh with her smell, erotically laced with his own.

CHAPTER
FORTY

WHEN THEY FINALLY pulled up outside the darkened gate, Emma couldn't see anything but the shadow of a blunt, square house.

"Well this is it," said Clayton.

Talia leaned forward and Emma heard her whisper, "Does she know?"

She suddenly felt too afraid to speak. She saw Clayton almost imperceptibly shake his head.

"It's been such a long time, Emma, and so much has happened, so, so much," said Clayton turning to her in the darkness. "I wanted to tell you everything but there never seemed an appropriate time. And this isn't one either. I'm going to go in and check for Calvin and, when I come out, we'll talk, I promise."

Before Emma could reply he was out the door, disappearing towards the shadowed house. She sat quietly for a moment or two, her arm resting on the steering wheel, peering into the distance. But she couldn't just sit there, her fears for Calvin and the tension between her and Talia growing. She glanced briefly back at Talia and stepped out of the car, following Clayton into the darkness.

And, as she did, she felt the panic bubbling in her chest, her bowels turning slowly to water.

CHAPTER
FORTY-ONE

1977

THE HARDEST TIMES were when David was home on leave. It was never more than a fortnight but it seemed to last forever. The moment he arrived Harry would be despatched back to his family. Frankly he was relieved to go, he couldn't bear to be so close to her and not be able to touch her.

So he would go home to face Gwennie and her increasing aggression, an instinctive reaction to an insecurity she could feel but not explain.

Those fortnights were a blur to him. He would try to focus on the family, take time to play football with Calvin, help Bernice with her homework, and cuddle baby Talia to sleep. But his mind and his thoughts and his heart were somewhere else.

He would lie awake for hours next to Gwennie, racked by guilt and desire and frustration. All he could think was that she was nothing like Margot.

Within hours of David reporting for duty at the army barracks, Harry would be back at the house. He would practically run down the driveway and grin like a lovelorn school boy when he spotted Margot standing and waiting for him on the porch. Then he would scoop her up in his arms and hold her tight, breathing her in as if his life depended on it.

After making love they'd lie in each other's arms, their limbs plaited, and talk. Harry had never talked to another human being as much as he'd talked to Margot. He wondered how it was possible that he'd had a marriage and three children, yet no-one knew him as well as this woman.

Margot opened up a floodgate of emotions and sensations in him. He found himself talking about all his hopes, his dreams, his squandered ambitions; a marriage made out of duty, not love; his fears for his children who he wanted to have a better life than his, but who were already trapped in a cycle they could probably never escape.

She would lie quietly and listen, gently running her hands through his soft curls, kissing the top of his head.

"What went wrong with David?" he once asked her.

She hesitated a moment before answering. "I was really young, wanted so badly to get away from my parents and their control." Harry lay behind her, his form melded into her back, his arms around her waist. Her face was turned towards the window, the light from the full moon a silver sheath. "David was handsome and charming and I genuinely thought he was the one. Maybe he was…then."

Her eyes dropped from the window to her fingers, laced through Harry's, and she squeezed them tight. "It worked while I was pliable, but when I started to voice my opinion, have my own ideas, it didn't go down so well with him. It doesn't go down so well with him. Our outlook on life, our view of the world, our politics, they're just so different. But when you're young and in love you don't notice all that, you don't think there's anything you can't work out. With hindsight, he didn't want a wife, he wanted a possession."

He gently turned her towards him and kissed her on her forehead, her cheek, her full mouth, trying to kiss away her pain...and his own. He tasted the salt of her tears as he kissed her closed eyelids.

CHAPTER
FORTY-TWO

THE HOUSE WAS silent and dark and Clayton's hard rapping on the wide wooden door rang sharply in the night.

There were muffled noises from inside and then footsteps.

A massive bear of a man flung open the door and filled the threshold. His dark hair was tousled, his jowls shadowy with stubble.

"What!" he said, making no attempt to mask his irritation. Then, recognising Clayton, added "Oh, it's you."

"Sorry Denzel, I know it's late, but it's important. Have you seen Calvin?"

"Jah, he's out back."

"Can I go through?"

"Please yourself, you know the way."

"How's the old man?"

"Same as always. The o' queen says he needs more medication and we gotta start getting him those nappies. He's shittin' all over the place and becoming a stinking mess."

"They're damn expensive, but I'll see what I can do. For now, though, I need to see Calvin."

He walked towards the back of the house, through the kitchen and into a small courtyard. Facing them was a small room, probably once the domestic quarters.

Hearing footsteps he turned around to see Emma coming up behind him.

"Emma! I thought..."

But he didn't get a chance to finish. Emma was looking past him, her eyes wide. The door to the small, shabby room was slightly ajar and Calvin was lying just inside it, in a pool of his own vomit. They rushed towards him and, as they did, Emma saw out of the corner of her eye a shadowy figure hunched in a wheelchair, shaking his grizzled head slowly from side to side and crying softly.

CHAPTER
FORTY-THREE

1977

THEY ONLY HAD one full glorious night together. It was the school holidays and the children were spending the night with friends. No sneaking to the back of the yard in the dead of night, no quiet whispering, no listening out to hear if one of the children was calling. For that one night nothing else mattered.

With all the excitement of a first date Margot dressed in a favourite floral wrap dress which exposed her creamy throat and skimmed her legs just below the knee; she cooked a special meal which they ate picnic style on the floor of the living room, then Harry lit a fire and they lay together in the warm glow. They didn't sleep at all that night, didn't want to miss a moment of it. They talked and made love throughout the night, finally falling into a deep sleep as the next-door neighbour's rooster heralded the dawn.

That was the first time Harry told her he loved her. He'd known it for a long time, but he'd been too afraid to say it until then.

"I love you," he said, nuzzling her neck, his voice thick with desire, "marry me."

She sat bolt upright and stared, startled, into his eyes. "What did you just say?"

"I said marry me."

"No, the other thing," she said and smiled.

"I love you. But then you already know that."

"Yes," she paused, then nodded decidedly, "I do."

"And?"

She smiled and ran her fingers across his brow. "I love you too, God I love you." And her voice broke.

Grinning, he said: "And the other thing?"

"What other thing?" she asked with a smile.

"Will you marry me?"

"Harry, if only." And the smile died on her lips.

"If only what?"

"If only, if only, too many to list."

"So that's a no, then?"

"You know it has to be."

"No, I don't know. All I know is that I love you more than I've ever loved anyone, that I'm willing to risk everything to be with you, that every moment away from you is torture."

She placed a finger gently on his lips.

"Not now," she said, her voice husky, "let's not think about it now. There'll be plenty of time for thinking tomorrow."

And she pulled him closer to her and silenced his half-hearted protests with her urgent kisses.

CHAPTER
FORTY-FOUR

FOR THE SECOND time in less than a week Emma found herself in the emergency ward.

Everything that happened after she and Clayton found Calvin lying unconscious on the floor was a haze. She knew there was someone else in the room, an elderly man, crying as he sat in a wheelchair. She was aware that Calvin was minutes away from death, his skin as pale as paper, his eyes rolled back in his head, a stream of vomit dribbling from the corner of his mouth.

She heard Clayton cry out as if it was coming from a long way away. There were hurried footsteps, people pushing, pressing forward, somewhere in the confusion Talia screaming.

Two men, one of them the grizzly bear who'd answered the door, lifted Calvin's limp body and carried him outside. Clayton was grabbing her hand and they were rushing to her car. The two men lay Calvin on the back seat next to Talia, who was sobbing loudly and stroking his head while Sabrina looked on, wide-eyed and confused.

Emma reversed up the driveway and sped to the hospital, Clayton shouting directions, and, as soon as they pulled up outside emergency, almost before the car stopped moving, Clayton leapt out. Moments later the hospital doors flew open and a stretcher was wheeled out. Calvin was lifted on to it, and disappeared through the doors.

All she could think as she paced the waiting room was that he hadn't been breathing. She'd placed her hand on his chest as he lay on the floor of the room but there was nothing.

Then she remembered another day, so many years ago, when she'd frantically searched for signs of life and found none. Now it was all coming back to her, clear as day, the memory that had nagged at her since she'd met Calvin.

And with painful clarity she saw once again the little boy with the huge green eyes and unruly mop of curls who'd run past her and Peter that horrific day, just moments after the shot was fired.

CHAPTER
FORTY-FIVE

1978

MARGOT HAD BEEN pregnant twice before, so it was no mystery to her when the nausea began. There was no mistaking the deep, hollow emptiness which gnawed hungrily at her belly, an emptiness that nothing could fill, the stiffness deep in her abdomen, like glass plates shifting.

Just as she knew with an unwavering certainty that she was pregnant, she knew it was Harry's. It wasn't just the dates that matched up, it was the deep, unbreakable bond that had linked him to her from the very beginning. And she felt the ties of that bond tugging as she placed her hand on her still flat belly, murmuring, in her imagination, with new life.

On one hand she felt a deep, overwhelming sense of love. On the other, intense, desperate panic. A married woman. Pregnant with another man's child. A Coloured man.

It was such a small, innocent thing Emma had said to her father that day. Meaningless to anyone else. At first, meaningless to David. Until, like lyrics you sing without thinking that slowly become the words to a song, it all began to make sense. The pieces of a puzzle began to shift and move in David's mind, forming, at last, a complete and horrifying picture.

He was in the van, reversing up the driveway, on his way back to the army after his two week leave. Emma ran breathlessly up the drive towards him to remind him it was her birthday and to tell him to ask the army for special leave. She was giggling and flushed.

All he could think was that he had to get back to the barracks, that he had no time for this. He was irritable and impatient, the growing tension between him and Margot beginning to wear him down. He made to leave and then Emma placed her hand on the window frame, looked intently into his eyes and said, "Don't worry, Daddy, Harry's here, Harry'll look after us while you're away. He always does."

He tried to keep his voice even when he told her to step back from the car. He had to go. But he could feel the strangeness in his voice, the strangeness in his head.

He continued reversing but his mind was distracted, and he misjudged the gate he had negotiated so many times he could practically do it blind-folded. A cold and unreasonable sensation clutched at his heart and spread through his chest. He pressed down hard on the steering wheel and accelerated onto the street. As he sped off his head was reeling. Harry will look after us. The chant echoed in his head like a funeral march all the way to the station, following him even as the train choked and trundled back into the bowels of hell.

Margot could hardly hear David's garbled words over the crackling line.

"Where are you David? Where are you calling from?"

"Margot, I know, God-dammit, I know! Emma told me!"

"What? David, I can't hear you properly, Emma told you what?"

And Emma, listening from the other room, shrank with fear and shame. What had she said? What had she done to make her mother sound so scared?

"David, we'll talk when you get home, I can hardly hear you, you're not making sense."

"You bitch, you and that fucking goffel! I know, I know! How could I have been so fucking blind?" And now he was sobbing uncontrollably.

"David, David, I don't understand what you're talking about." But Emma could hear the panic in her mother's voice and knew something bad was about to happen.

"I'm on my way back, I've asked for compassionate leave. Just wait 'till I get my hands on that fucking piece of shit! It's all falling into place now. How could I have been so stupid?

When Margot put down the phone she was white and shaking.

"Mommy?" Emma's voice was small and breathless.

Margot, startled, looked around. She hadn't realised Emma had been listening. She struggled to control her shaking hands and reached out and held the little girl tight.

"Don't worry, honey, everything's going to be fine." But her shaking voice and hands belied her. "Sweetheart, did you say something to Daddy about Harry?"

"About Harry? No Mama," she said, pulling away slightly to look up at her mother. "Oh, I just said Daddy shouldn't worry about us coz Harry'll look after us. Mama, that's all I said, did I do something bad? Harry does look after us when Daddy's away, doesn't he?"

"Yes, honey, he does. And, no, you've done nothing bad, nothing wrong. Everything's going to be fine," she repeated, as much for her own reassurance as Emma's.

Harry was working at the home of a wealthy family on the other side of town. It was a big contract and he was ecstatic; the fact that he'd found the work the day Margot had told him about the baby was, to him, a good omen. They were going to make it.

He caught a ride from the city centre out to the big house at 5 each morning and although he was happy to leave the Hardy's as early as 4 to make the pick-up time, that week Talia had been running a high fever and he and Margot had decided it would be best he stay at home for a few days.

When he was called from his building work into the house to take a phone call, he was surprised and a little anxious. His first thought was Talia.

But instead of Gwennie's voice on the other end of the line it was Margot, breathless and gasping.

"Harry, he knows, David knows! Lord, Harry, what are we going to do? He's on his way back to town!"

"My love, it's OK, try to calm down, this could be the best thing. You know we had to tell him eventually."

"But not like this, not yet, Harry, not now!"

"I'm finishing here and getting a ride home. Meet me at the lot behind the apartment, please darling, just meet me there. We'll talk about it, we'll make a plan."

"Oh Harry, will it be OK? Are you sure it's going to be OK?" She was trying to soak up Harry's confidence and strength, so tangible even through the distant telephone lines.

"Yes baby, it's going to be OK. Meet me there in 20 minutes' time."

"But I have the children with me, and there's no-one to leave them with."

"Just come past quickly, just let me hold you and kiss you and reassure you it'll be OK. You'll be there?"

"Yes, I'll be there." A pause, then she added, "Wherever you are, I'll be there."

And he smiled. "I love you."

Margot put down the phone and managed, for the first time since David's call, to calm her shaking hands and ragged breathing. She'd spoken to Harry and everything was going to be alright.

Then she told the children to pack away their toys, they had to go out.

CHAPTER
FORTY-SIX

Emma 1978

THE SKY THAT day was all rippled, soft wavy clouds that looked like beach sand when the tide goes out.

Peter and I were in the back seat of the car and we were fighting. I just wanted to see Peter's new dinky car but he wouldn't let me.

No, he said, you'll break it, and he was holding it tight and turned away from me so I couldn't get it.

I told him I wouldn't but he said I would and that I broke his last one.

He knew that wasn't my fault and I told him then I got angry and tried to grab it from him.

He said no again and shoved my hand away.

Peter never shoved me before and I got sad and mad all at once so I yelled and told Mommy that he hit me. He said he hadn't, I said yes he had, Mommy, he hit me.

But Mommy didn't answer. That's when I noticed she was leaning forward in the car seat, hanging on to the steering wheel and holding it tight. She didn't look like Mommy.

She was driving fast and she sped through an orange light which she never did.

I pressed up against the back of her seat and said Mommy, Mommy didn't you hear me, I said Peter hit me.

Yes, Emma, she said, I heard you. I knew she was trying to sound like she always did but she didn't. She sounded funny like someone was pinching her throat so the words wouldn't come out.

I asked her if she was going to shout at him, that it was sore… and I stuck my elbow through the gap in the seats to show her.

Then Peter started shouting, calling me a liar, and then he hit me for real.

Calvin had waited all day for his father to come home and play football with him. Every couple of hours he'd ask his mother and every time she'd give him the same response: "I fuckin' told you he's coming home later!"

Finally he heard the familiar sound of the pick-up truck which dropped his father off on nights when he wasn't sleeping over at the Hardy's, and he raced to the street.

"Dad, Dad, where you been?" He was laughing, grabbing his father around the waist and swinging his feet off the floor.

Harry lifted him up with one arm, held him up so his face was close to his own and planted a kiss on his flushed cheek.

"Hey, my boy, what's happening?"

"Nothin' Dad, been waiting for you to jol cabin all day. Ma keeps saying you coming then you don't show."

"Waiting for me to come home, Calvin, what's this 'jol cabin', huh? When did you start talking slang? Speak properly my boy, that's what I'm always telling you, you'll never get through school speaking slang."

"Aw Dad, this is how all my chinas – I mean all my friends – talk."

"Well it's not the way you're going to talk, do you hear me? You're going to make something of yourself, my boy, I know you are. I've got a good feeling about our future, Calvin, I have a feeling our fortunes are about to change," and Calvin had never seen his father look so excited, beaming like a school boy.

He chuckled with delight and threw his arms around his father's neck.

"Come on Dad, play football with me, I wanna show you my new moves."

"I will, my boy, I will, but first there's something important I have to do. You go on in and wait for me, I'll be with you just now."

"Promise Dad?" And the little boy's eyes were wide as Harry put him down.

"Yes, my boy, I promise," said Harry, getting down on one knee and looking deep into his son's eyes. "I know I may not have been around a lot lately and I'm sorry about that. I want you to know that whatever happens I love you, my boy. I love you and your sisters so much."

"And Ma."

Harry swallowed hard then pulled his son close, burying his face in the soft, wayward curls. "And Ma."

He stood up and watched as Calvin raced back into the courtyard, kicking up dust as he ran, then made his way down the sidewalk towards the empty lot on the other side of the apartment block.

Calvin ran as far as the apartment steps then remembered he wanted to tell his Dad about the sticker he got from his teacher for good sums, so he ran back out onto the street and saw Harry rounding the corner at the end of the block.

He ran inside to deposit his beloved football in the apartment then made off after him.

Emma

The minute I started crying, Peter said he was sorry he'd done it.

Sorry, Emma, sorry, I didn't mean to hit you he said. But I was too sad to say it was OK so I told him yes he did mean to do it even though I really knew inside that he didn't.

He was trying really hard to make up. Come on, he said, don't be like that, I'm trying to say sorry.

By now, with all the noise and fussing, Mommy was swivelling around in the driver's seat, trying to pat me on the arm to make me feel better and tell Peter off and watch the road all at the same time.

You two are going to make me have an accident, she said and she told us to stop our silliness! She told Peter to say sorry to me and told me to stop my crying.

He told her he did say sorry but I wouldn't listen, and I told Mommy that was because he always hit me. That wasn't true either but I was sad and angry and I didn't even really know why.

Mommy also said it wasn't true, she said no, he never hit me and I went quiet. Then she asked us to please be quiet and behave. She said it was too much now and she sounded like she really meant it.

We both went quiet, sitting on our own sides of the car, looking out of the window.

After a little while of being quiet and looking out the window Peter asked Mommy where we were going.

Mommy said we were going to Harry's apartment, that there was something she had to tell him.

Straight away I got that funny feeling in my tummy again and I asked Mommy if it was because of what I said that made Daddy mad.

Peter didn't know about Daddy being mad and he asked mad about what.

Mommy's voice went all soft and she said no one was mad, no one was mad, but her saying it twice made me think someone was really mad. Then she said what she always said to make bad things seem better, she said everything would be fine.

But I looked at Peter and knew from his face and by Mommy's voice that it wouldn't be.

Mommy stopped outside a high grey wall. There were old, broken down buildings on one side and a big bushy field on the other. We couldn't see any other cars or people. I didn't like it. I was scared.

Mommy turned to the back and told Peter to lock the doors and make sure I stayed in the car. She said she'd be back soon.

Peter asked her where she was going and his voice was shaky.

I told Mommy I was scared, in a little voice that wouldn't come out.

She leant over and ran her fingers through my hair, like she did some nights when I was lying in bed and scared and couldn't sleep. There's nothing to be scared of, she said. She said she'd be back in a minute, she'd just tell Harry something important and then she'd come straight back. Then she said we'd go home and put the finishing touches to my cake. That made me a little happier. I'd almost forgotten it was my birthday. She said who's going to be a big 10 year old tomorrow and I said, I am.

She told us not to worry, to wait there and she'd be back soon. Then she got out the car and started to walk to the grey wall. We were watching her go and then suddenly she turned around and came back and said with her lips only "I love you". Before we could say we loved her too she turned and started walking again.

Watching Mommy walking through that giant gate didn't feel good at all. I slid along the seat to Peter and we sat close, waiting, and not saying anything.

David had finally managed to get through to Margot from the army barracks at the edge of the city. He'd tried countless times from the phone at the camp but without success. As he sat at the barracks waiting for his release papers to be signed, he couldn't contain his panic and fear and anger any longer and asked to use the phone and try Margot one last time.

He didn't think to tell her he was already in town. She presumed from the bad connection that he was still far away.

He pulled up at the house minutes after Margot had driven off. The Johnson children, playing outside the next door gate told him, pointed out the direction the family had taken.

David caught sight of the boxy blue Datsun as it turned off Hillcrest Avenue, heading into town. He pulled back and followed at a reasonable distance.

Their father was the last person the children expected to see. His car pulled up alongside them minutes after their mother had walked through the gates.

"Daddy!" said Emma as he walked up to the car and Peter unlocked the door.

He was flushed and out of breath. "Where's your mother?"

"There," said Emma, pointing at the walled yard. She was confused and alarmed by his dishevelled appearance.

He said nothing more, slammed the door shut and strode purposefully towards the gate. She wanted to call out, to tell him to wait, but the words caught in her throat.

She started to cry again and Peter, not needing to ask why, put his arm around her and held her close.

Calvin squeezed through a hole in the fence he and his friends had discovered and scrambled onto a pile of gravel at the edge of the lot. From this vantage point he could see his father, quite far away and with his back turned to him. With a White woman. He had his arms around her and was kissing her on the forehead. He almost called out but then clapped his hand over his mouth and just stood there.

He watched as the stranger cupped his father's face with her hands, smiled, and held him close.

Then the urgent thud of footsteps entering the yard. They all turned in unison, Harry and Margot pulling abruptly apart. But it was too late. David Hardy, hair tousled, eyes wild, cheeks flushed crimson, had already seen them.

Calvin watched the tragedy unfold wide-eyed, so afraid his feet were rooted to the ground for what seemed like forever.

Emma

It went so quiet after Daddy went through the big black gate after Mommy. And we just kept waiting, not saying a word. Then came the bang! I jumped so high, I'd never heard a sound like it, like a huge firework or the sound grandpa's car sometimes used to make. But I think Peter had heard that kind of sound and he knew what it was because his eyes went wide, his hands went to his head and he started to shout.

Before I knew what was happening he unlocked the car door and started running really, really fast to the gate. I was starting to cry and didn't know what to do, so I opened my side of the car and started running after him.

Peter was already running back when I got there, his face was so scared my whole tummy went funny like I wanted to go to the toilet. He ran to me and reached out and pulled at me trying to make me stop from going in and seeing but it was too late. I looked and I saw. I saw Mommy and Daddy and Harry and I started screaming but it didn't sound like it was coming from me, it sounded like it was coming from someone else. Peter pulled me to him and tried to push my head into his shoulder but it was too late. I saw. Harry was lying over Mommy and I could see blood. He had a gun in his hand and he was crying like an animal. Howling like our boerboel puppy, Jacko, howled that time the snake bit him and then he died. He was saying I killed her, I killed her. Daddy was on his knees, he was holding his head in his hands and Daddy was sobbing like a baby.

That was when I saw him, the scruffy barefoot boy with wide green eyes and black curls, running from behind where Mommy was lying, past her and Peter and me and into the street. I don't really remember but I think I was still screaming.

CHAPTER
FORTY-SEVEN

CLAYTON LIGHTLY TOUCHED Emma's arm and she jumped.

"Oh Clayton, it's you."

"Emma dear, are you OK? You're as white as a sheet."

"I'm fine, I'm fine. How's Calvin? Is there news?"

"Yes, the doctors say he's regained consciousness. We can go in and see him."

"Oh thank God," and her deep sense of relief surprised her.

Calvin was lying back on a pair of plump pillows, an intricate labyrinth of drips pumping life back into his veins.

His eyes were closed when they walked in but, hearing movement, he opened them slightly.

They came up on either side of him and Emma rested her hand on his cold arm.

"Hi, how you feeling?"

"Like shit," he said, then closed his eyes again.

"Are you tired, son, do you want to sleep?" asked Clayton.

He nodded his head slightly. "Was planning to take a long, long dos," his voice was just a murmur. "Heard some bozos came in and interrupted it."

Emma didn't trust herself to speak.

He opened his eyes and looked at Emma, managed a weak smile out of the corner of his mouth and then closed them again, exhausted.

"We're going to leave you to rest, son, but we'll be back."

He didn't reply and Emma gently squeezed his arm before following Clayton out the door.

CHAPTER
FORTY-EIGHT

WHEN EMMA ANSWERED the phone in her hotel room the following evening she immediately recognised Talia's voice on the other end.

"This is Talia."

"Hi Talia, how's Calvin?"

Her voice was cold. "He's asking for you."

"For me?" She could hardly hide the surprise in her voice. "OK, thanks, I was going to go around there in the morning anyway – was just giving him a day to rest."

"Right," and Talia made to hang up.

"Talia," she paused uncertainly, "are you OK?" She wanted to talk to her, tell her so many things, but when Talia replied with a very final and uninviting "I'm fine," she lost her nerve, said goodbye and put down the phone.

The next morning Emma was relieved to see Calvin sitting up in bed, still pale and drawn but much more alert than the last time she'd seen him.

"You joled," was all he said, then indicated for her to take a seat in the chair next to his bed.

He sat silently for a few minutes, leaned his head back against the pillows, closed his eyes, and then, without preamble, began.

"I scheme you think it was a pretty shit thing I did?" he held up his hand to silence her when she started to protest. "Jah, it was shit, jah it was stupid, but, fuck, I was just so tired of all the shit, just spans and spans of shit that seems to follow me wherever I jol.

"Then the o' queen dying, that was it, man! Dying and I wasn't even fuckin' there. I didn't have a big plan, I just knew I was so, so tired of all the shit and if I dossed, like for a span, forever maybe, it would all go away." He ran his right hand through his hair, making the curls stand up on end.

"So I joled from the hospital but didn't want to jol cabin, didn't want to see nothing that reminded me of her. I joled to Harry's cabin, my o' man, my fucked up o' man. I scheme you thought he was dead, menses all think he is. Sometimes wish he was, be better than what he is now, so fucked up.

"Drank 'till I couldn't drink no more, Harry watching me the whole time, moaning. Felt lekker, that numb feeling, schemed it might be a lekker idea to make the numbness last. I joled to the medicine cabinet and took a handful of my o' man's painkillers, crammed them into my mouth, so many my mouth was full, my cheeks bulging, a few even fell out. But got enough of 'em down with a swig of good o' Mr Jack Daniels. And then waited for the fuckin' pain to stop." He leaned back against the pillows and closed his eyes.

Emma said nothing.

"Ya want answers," he said, lifting his head up off the pillows and snapping his eyes open. "Ya joled here for answers. So I'm gonna oblige. Then maybe ya can jol cabin and get on with your fuckin' life. Instead of throwing it all away coz of somethin' went down so long ago no-one even remembers, no-one gives a shit about anymore.

"I was there," he said.

"Yes. I know. I remember," Emma said, meeting his eyes.

1978

"So this is what you want, you slut?" David screamed. "This is really what you want? A fucking goffel bastard! You bitch! You fucking bitch! Fucking a goffel! A goffel! How could you!"

Harry jumped in front of Margot, spreading out his arms to shield her.

"Please, Mr Hardy, please, just calm down for a moment, let's be reasonable, let's talk about this," said Harry.

"There's nothing to fucking talk about! Get away from my wife, you fucking goffel!"

"David, David, please don't do this," Margot's voice was frantic.

"Shut up!" he screamed, "Shut up both of you!"

Harry saw David reach into his pocket and knew what it held. He gently but insistently pushed Margot away from him, away from the line of fire, and even as the silver barrel of the gun was pulled free of his pocket and winked in the dying sunlight, Harry was rounding on him.

"I'll show you! I'll fucking show both of you!" howled David.

Harry sprinted forward, throwing himself at him as he pulled back the trigger. The force of the tackle took the wind out of David and flung his hand sideways, changing the fatal course of the bullet.

Harry was grabbing the gun from David's tightly-clenched hand as Margot fell. His mind couldn't comprehend what his eyes were seeing. Smeared in dust and sweat, mind reeling, the gun still in his hand, he ran to where her crumpled body lay and threw himself on her, cradling her head and howling, repeating over and over again "I killed her! Oh my God! Oh my love! I killed her!"

"Those were the last proper words my o' man praated," said Calvin. "I saw you standing there that day, I heard ya scream, ya bro was pushing ya face against his shoulder so ya wouldn't see. I ran past ya and kept on running. I scheme I been running ever since.

"My o' queen schemes I hardly praated for a year after it happened. S'pose there didn't seem like there was nothin' worth praating about. Jah, I was scared. Jah I schemed if I didn't praat about it, it'd be like it never happened.

"I was just a lightie for fuck's sake, didn't know 'bout legal crap 'n stuff. Wen they put my o' man away, said he killed some married White chick he was fucking, wat was I gonna say? Who was gonna listen? We became known as the murderer's lighties, kids teased us 'n called us names, parents warned their lighties to stay away from us. It didn't last, soon there was some new scandal to occupy everyone, but it was crap while it lasted. 'N me not praating at all. But that was nothin' compared to all the other shit that went down, my o' man gone, my fuckin' stepfather, my o' queen, turning into a drunken hoe."

"Only years later I told Talia 'n Uncle Clay. Wat was they gonna do? Wat was anyone gonna do?"

1978

After Margot's death, Harry was half out of his mind, garbling and groaning incoherently.

His defence lawyers, hired for him by the state, had nothing to work with.

Then there was his self-confession at the scene of the crime and no other witnesses.

When David finally gathered himself together that day, he phoned for back-up. He phoned Lawrence, a friend who'd served in the police and, later, with David in the security forces. Once the children had been driven away to safety, the two set to work to re-construct the crime.

In all fairness to David, he was too shocked and ravaged with grief to spin any stories. Lawrence had taken him firmly by the shoulders and shaken him hard.

"Do you want to fry, David? Because as God is my witness,

that's what's going to happen if anyone finds out you fired the shot! Is that really what you want? Grab a hold of yourself, man!"

David just shook his head from side to side.

By the time the court case came around he had pulled himself together and, rehearsed with the close guidance of Detective Lawrence Spencer, managed to paint a very convincing picture of the grieving widower, tortured by the death of his wife at the hands of her Coloured lover, a contract worker employed by the family.

His lawyer's opening statement reiterated the lie.

"Harry Rhoades was pressurising Margot Hardy to leave her husband and run away with him, and urged her to meet him at a deserted lot near his apartment. When David Hardy came home unexpectedly from army duty and caught the two of them together, a scuffle broke out, during which Rhoades produced a gun which he aimed at Hardy. The court will hear how Mrs Hardy, fearing for her husband's life, threw herself in front of him and took the bullet to her chest. She died instantly."

David sat on the witness stand and told the court how he had suspected the two were having an affair and confronted his wife about it in a telephone call on his way back from duty on compassionate leave. He had a very strong sense from the telephone call that his wife was repentant, ready to end the affair.

"She must have told Rhoades I was on my way back and he pressured her to meet him."

"Why do you think he had a gun on him? Had you threatened Harry Rhoades in any way, given him cause for fear?" probed his lawyer.

"No, no of course not. How could I? I had only just realised what was going on. I can't really say why he was carrying a gun. He knew I was coming home, perhaps anticipated trouble, was going to take what he wanted at any cost," and even though the defence leapt up and interjected with an insistent 'overrule', David had had his say.

The police department had always been vaguely aware of the discrepancies in the case, suspicious that there had been some kind of cover-up, some question as to whom the gun – mysteriously missing from the evidence bag – belonged. Extenuating circumstances no-one had ever examined.

So when, almost 15 years later, Calvin pressed for the case to be appealed, and with a new government in power, it was relatively easy to get Harry released.

In the tumult and confusion of a transitional government, the court papers, riddled with inconsistencies, were nowhere to be found. David Hardy was long since dead. So was Detective Spencer.

"It's all in the past, don't ya get that?" Calvin was almost shouting. "They're all gone, dead!" Then his voice went quiet again. "My o' man was outta that hell hole, for me that was all that mattered."

"And now?" asked Emma in a small voice, her face streaked with tears. "What matters now?"

"Shit matters now," he said. "I scheme that's the problem."

They sat in silence for a long time. Then he stirred. "Scheme ya probably thinks I'm lying."

She didn't answer.

"Don't really give a shit either way," he said, pulling out a yellowed sheet of paper, a mass of creases from being constantly touched and folded and re-folded. "It's yours if ya want it, I'm done with it, done with all of it."

He tossed it into her lap.

"That day I joled to the Calderwoods I wasn't lookin' for graft, I was lookin' for ya o' man. I was gonna kill him. Instead found this sweet o' queen willin' to treat me like a human being, not like some dirty goffel brat.

"I was gonna kill him for what he did to my o' man, to my whole family. Only found out later he'd done the job for me, got himself killed in the war all on his own. Or killed himself, no-one knows, no-one ever will. All I cared about was that he was dead and I prayed day and night he was rotting in hell."

Emma winced but he was unapologetic.

"Rotting in fucking hell," he repeated.

"Now if it's OK with you, I'm tired, I need to dos." And he closed his eyes as she stood up, the piece of paper in her hands, and left the ward, her feet unsteady, her eyes blurry from all the crying.

She walked outside and sat on a bench close to the hospital building, then opened the letter and began to read.

My darling Harry,

I tossed and turned all through the night trying to figure out what to do. I've woken up with one very strong realisation: I love you Harry, I never imagined I could love anyone as much as I love you. I don't know how we'll do it, I don't know what will become of us, but I'm not giving you or this baby up. I'm ready to leave David and be with you, if you'll have me and the children. He goes back to the army next week, I can't wait to see you, my love, to plan the adventure of our lives together.

Always yours,

Margot

Emma realised, for the first time in 30 years, she'd always known.

CHAPTER
FORTY-NINE

EMMA HAD A few hours to spare before driving to the airport to check in for her flight.

She pulled up at number 17 and hooted, then watched as Calvin, walking slowly but steadily, came to the gate and unlocked it for her. As she drove in, he raised his hand in greeting and gave her his characteristic sideways smile.

She stepped out of the car and, almost without thinking, greeted him with a hug. He hesitated for just a moment, then patted her awkwardly on the back before pulling away.

"You're looking great!"

"Shit, but you're a lekker liar."

"Well it's all relative, remember – I've seen you at your worst."

"Huh! Ya scheme that was my worst? Ya obviously didn't see me after my month-long bender with my chinas a few years back. We decided to extend New Year's into February…bad idea."

She laughed, following him out of the sun and on to the porch where they sat opposite each other on the garden chairs as they'd done on her first night there, what seemed like a lifetime ago.

"So, wat's the plan?" he asked, looking at her.

She smiled at him. "The plan is to go back to the States and try to pick up the pieces of my life, for what it's worth."

"You going back to ya o' man?"

"Just long enough to tell him everything and suggest we file for a divorce. I don't think it will be a big surprise to him."

"So ya chosen your dude?" Two short weeks ago he would have spat out the words. Now all he sounded was oddly disappointed.

"No Calvin, not chosen 'my dude' either. For once in my life I've chosen myself. I think I need to be alone for a while. I've been hiding behind something all my life. It helped when I was trying to hide from the past, you know, have a shield, but I don't think I need it anymore. Besides," she said, smiling sadly, "I don't have any of it to hide behind anymore: no job, no husband, no lover, just me. I guess, for once, that's OK."

"Ya sure?"

"Yes, I am," she said, crossing her long legs and leaning forward, an elbow resting on the table between them. "You know, Calvin, my mother and your father really loved each other. I don't think you or I have come close to feeling that kind of love in our lives. The way she was willing to keep the baby and risk it all for him, the way he was going to stand by her, no matter what society said. I don't condone the cheating, the destruction of our families but, God knows, with our past experiences, can we really judge them?"

She paused slightly, looking at him. "But they were courageous at the end, ready to do the right thing. You could have been my step-brother, Calvin, have you ever thought of that?"

"Jah, it haunts my nightmares, an uptight White chick for a step-ster," he said, shaking his head. Emma laughed.

Then she grew serious again. "That baby would have been our half sister or brother," she said, then dropped her eyes and looked down at the floor. "I fell pregnant about three months ago. Alan's baby. I had an abortion, Calvin, I made a mistake but didn't have the guts to make it right. I'm nothing at all like my mother." Her eyes were filling with tears.

"That really what ya scheme?" He looked at her and then sighed. "Chill here, I got somethin' for ya." He stood up and walked stiffly into the house.

He came back holding the painting of Margot in his hands.

"Unless my o' man was a really crap artist – and I know he wasn't – you're every bit your o' queen's lightie."

He held it out to her and as she took it from him the tears began to fall.

"Oh for fuck's sake, ya not gonna hub again are ya?"

She wiped furiously at her eyes and breathed in deeply, "Last time, Calvin, last time, I promise. Besides I'm going to be 10 000 miles away and then you're going to miss my hubbing."

"Jah maybe," he said, going suddenly quiet, "maybe."

"And what about your plans?" she said, holding the painting to her chest. "Is it safe to leave you alone or are you planning to turn this place into a Playboy mansion the minute I turn my back?"

"So ya heard she left me the cabin?"

"Yes, I did, and I'm so happy for you."

"Don't scheme I'll have much chance to fool around, Talia and Sabrina are moving in with me on the weekend. If I thought ya was a pain in the ass, it was only coz I'd forgotten what it was like living with my little ster." But his eyes were shining as he said it. "Hopefully once they're settled, I'll get my o' man here too."

"Oh Calvin, that's amazing, I can't believe it! Elizabeth would have been so happy."

His voice grew quiet. "Ya scheme?"

"I know. Where are Talia and Sabrina now?"

"At the back, Sabrina smaaks the mulberries."

Emma smiled.

It was time to go and they both stood and started walking slowly towards the car. Then Emma turned and looked at him.

"There's just one more thing, that first night, when you called my brother a…"

He cut her off mid-sentence, grimacing, "Shit, is there no time off for good behaviour? Soz, OK? I shouldn't have said it!"

"No, Calvin, that's not it! I'm just asking because I wondered how you knew."

His face relaxed, then he thrust his hands deep into his trouser pockets and looked down at the floor. Slowly he raised his eyes to meet hers again.

"Cause we, um, we kind of had a thing."

"What? Oh my God!" Her hand flew to her mouth.

"Hey it was a one-off!" he added, holding up the palms of his hands.

"That's not it – but when? How? I don't understand."

"Ya bro was here. Peter was here. About 10 years ago. The Calderwoods was overseas on holiday, it was just me in the cabin. He came, same like ya did, wanting to find out stuff. He aksed me not to tune anyone he was here, I schemed he'd at least 'av told ya."

"Peter and I have hardly spoken in 20 years. After my Mom was killed he withdrew from everything, everyone, including me. I guess we all have our coping mechanisms." She was walking towards the car again, the key jingling softly in her hand. "But last year, out of the blue, I got a Christmas card from him and Clive, his partner." She'd reached the car and put one hand up on the bonnet and turned around to face Calvin again. "But you and Peter, who would have thought…?"

"Jah I know! Hey, I was young, it was kinda an experiment," he said, a couple of steps behind her. "Not a very successful one either, judging by my sexual history since then." He smiled his lop-sided smile, gently removing the keys from her hand and unlocking the car door for her.

"You showed him the box." It was a statement, not a question. Now she understood the extra care taken over the anniversary cards, tying them lovingly together in a lavender ribbon.

Calvin opened the car door and swung it open for her. "He didn't wanna take nothing, said he'd leave it as it was."

"You told him everything?"

"Jah, he's the one tuned me I should appeal my o' man's case, even lent me some sheets for the legal fees, probably never 'av done it if it wasn't for him."

"I guess he thought I wouldn't be able to handle the truth about my father. And maybe, all those years ago, I wouldn't."

"And now?"

"I'm working on it." And she smiled sadly.

Emma held back the tears as she hugged him good-bye. She didn't shed a tear as he told her to come back some time. She was even dry-eyed when she jumped into her car and watched him wave to her from the drive-way of her childhood home for the last time.

Then, just as she rounded the corner, leaving Calvin, the house, her past behind, she sobbed like her heart would break the whole half hour drive to the airport.

CHAPTER FIFTY

THE PHONE WAS answered by a male voice after three short, sharp rings.

"Hello."

Her voice was unsteady. "Peter?"

"No, would you like to talk to him?"

"Yes please."

Muffled voices and the sound of the phone being passed to someone else.

"Hello?" a hint of uncertainty.

"Peter?"

"Yes?"

"Peter, it's Emma!"

"Emma? Emma! Where are you calling from? Is everything alright?"

"Yes, Peter, everything's alright. Great in fact. I'm in Seattle. I've been home, Peter, I think we need to talk."

"Oh God Emma," he said, his voice breaking, "I thought you'd never ask."

Glossary of slang

Aks – ask
A span – a lot
Bra – brother/dude
Cabin – home/house
China – friend
Cut – leave
Dos – sleep
Goffel – Coloured person/person of mixed race
Graft - work
Graze – food/eat
Gun 'em – beat them up
Huck – steal
Jah ('j' pronounced 'y') – yes
Jol – go/come/party
Lekker – nice/cool/good
Lightie – child/youngster

Makarad – Coloured person/person of mixed race
Mal - crazy
Menses – people
O' bali, o' man – father/husband
O' queen – mother/wife
Ouen – person/man
Praat – talk
Pump 'em up – beat them up
Scheme – think
Sheets – money
Smaak – like/enjoy
Sut – no
Tune – tell
Wheels - car
Ya – you

ABOUT THE AUTHOR

VIOLETTE SOHAILI KEE-TUI was born in Bulawayo, Zimbabwe. She began her journalism career as an 18-year-old school leaver, training as an apprentice journalist on a local magazine before going on to work for a national newspaper as, initially, a junior reporter on the news desk. But she didn't last there long - her love for feature writing and her distaste for politics did not go unnoticed by her superiors and she was quickly transferred to the features desk where she rose to the position of Assistant Features Editor. During her time in the national media she won several awards, most notably Feature Writer of the Year in the National Journalism Awards. She returned to her studies after four years of working in the field, receiving an Honours Diploma from the London School of Journalism.

Driven by the need to tell the stories of people and communities, Violette became what some would call a narrative journalist – which should have been a natural progression to fiction writing. However, it wasn't until her mid-30s that she wrote and submitted her first short story – to the Intwasa Short Story Competition – for which she won third place. The next year she would take second prize in the same competition and, in 2012, first place, winning the highly coveted Yvonne Vera Award.

While a full-time working mom, Violette began writing *Mulberry Dreams* as part of NANOWRIMO (National Novel Writing Month), an initiative held every November to encourage creative writing by setting a target of writing 50 000 words in one month. By the last day of the month Violette posted her submission: 50 003 words in total! It would take another 20 000-odd words and multiple revisions to get it to its present form. A mother of two, Emil and Katya, she still lives in her hometown of Bulawayo. She continues to use her journalism training in the spheres of marketing, media, communication training, community outreach, PR and freelance writing. She and her partner, Paul Hubbard, own a gift and art shop in Bulawayo, and together run historical and cultural tours and activities in the city.